U0139058

進階
法學英文

從比較台美法律講起

五南圖書出版公司 印行

楊崇森／著

自序

★ ★ ★

近年來高考司法官與律師考試增列法學英文一科，惜坊間似尚無有系統適於應考之參考書。學生每以準備為苦。本書作者高考司法官律師出身，早年公費留美，在紐約大學攻讀英美法獲得三個學位，且先後獲聯合國技術協助獎補金、美國學術團體聯合會暨佛爾布萊特基金會等獎助，多次赴美考察，並在哈佛與哥倫比亞等大學研修，曾在大學及研究所講授英美法及英文法學名著多年，法學著作繁多。十年前復著有《遨遊美國法》一書三冊，為國內探討英美法最深入最有趣之書籍。近年來作者因鑒於法學英文尚無適當參考書，考生準備倍感吃力，為免青年人經歷作者昔日研讀英美法摸索之苦，爰不顧辛勞與代價，又窮數月之久，稿經數易，始撰成本書，其特色如下：

一、本書共十一章，包括美國憲法，契約法、侵權行為法、物權法、親屬繼承法、公司法、證券法、刑法、民事訴訟法、刑事訴訟法及法律倫理等。中英文對照，目的在提升讀者法學英文之程度與對英文法學之理解，備供法律等系所學生研讀英美法，並應考國家考試之用，當然亦可供社會人士了解英美法之用。由於中美法律體系與內容出入太大，故本書著重英美法（尤其美國法）之闡釋，我國法則從旁居於補充比較地位，以免浪費篇幅與讀者時力。

　　二、本書敘述力求簡潔明快，有系統有條理，使讀者能了解英美法各領域之全貌與抓住其法制之重點，且不囿於理論，更兼顧其實務運作，使讀者不致有見樹而不見森林，支離破碎或不知所云之感。

　　三、本書比較美國法與我國法特色，使讀者了解雙方精神根本之差異，並略提各領域美國法之源流，使讀者對美國法制之精神與運作有深一層之體會，更能透過比較，強化讀者對英美法之理解，此點為本書難寫之處，但亦為本書之特長。

　　四、各章除正文外，尚列有詳細中英文對照之詞彙，並附上豐富之習題（選擇題）與答案，俾便讀者研習之用。

　　五、各章之後除列有習題外，並附上相關的動詞換名詞、名詞換動詞、名詞動詞換形容詞、同義詞、異義詞、反義詞等，俾讀者多方接觸英文法學術語，期能觸類旁通，易於記憶，培養熟練法學英文詞彙之能力。

　　本書之成，諸承許多親友鼓勵，包括學棣臺北大學法律學院院長郭玲惠、日月光公司行政長汪渡村博士、陳逢源律師、李佩昌律師、黃婉柔小姐等之協助，五南公司劉靜芬副總編輯暨林佳瑩編輯之合作，在此併誌謝忱。

楊崇森
識於台北 2023年5月1日勞動節

CONTENTS

目錄　CONTENTS

目錄　CONTENTS

第一章	憲法

第一節　美國法

一、介紹

Various legal issues are involved with Constitution. This is especially true in the U.S. where the Constitution permeates into every sphere of society. People often bring lawsuits on the grounds that their constitutional rights are being violated.

憲法涉及各種法律問題，尤其在美國，憲法更滲透各種領域，民眾常以違憲為名提起訴訟。

美國憲法之主要內容：

（一）Republican Government 共和政體

The U.S. Constitution is the first written constitution in the world. It adopted a republican form of government and aimed to limit the power of government and secure the liberty of citizens.

美國憲法為世界最早之成文憲法，採用共和政體，旨在限制政府之權力，保障人民之自由。

（二）Checks and Balances 三權制衡

It adopted the doctrine of legislative, executive, and judicial separation of powers, the checks and balances of each branch against the others.

採立法、行政、司法三權分立與制衡。[*]

*三權之關係：

1. 司法與行政：法官由總統任命。尤其最高法院法官由於屬於保守派或自由派，左右判決結果，且影響社會重大。過去總統與法院常有衝突，總統利用任命大法官之權力，以控制法院，例如羅斯福總統因新政被宣告無效，亟欲將該法院改組。
2. 立法對司法：聯邦法院，除了最高法院外，係基於法律之規定而成立但法院可宣告違憲之法律無效。
3. 行政對立法：詳後。

（三）Legislative Branch 立法權

Congress consists of Senate (2 member for each state) and House of Representatives (based upon the population of each state), with powers to make laws, collect taxes, regulate inter-state commerce, declare war, etc. The president can be impeached by the House of Representatives and tried by the Senate.

國會由參議院（每州兩名）與眾議院（按各州人口）所組成。國會有權立法、徵稅、規範州際通商、宣戰等*。總統可由眾議院彈劾，參議院審判。

*國會只能透過彈劾程序免去行政官吏。國會雖有宣戰權，但實際上總統之軍事權力遠多於國會，且可用指揮軍隊權創造戰爭情況，迫使國會宣戰，也可以外交政策導致加入戰爭。

（四）Executive Power 行政權

The executive power is vested in the president who is elected by the people. He command the armed forces, can sign or veto laws, make treaties and grant pardons. He appoints cabinet members and federal judges subject to senate's consent.

行政權歸屬於由人民選出*之聯邦總統**。總統擔任三軍統帥，有權簽署或否決法律、締結條約及赦免。總統經參議院同意，任命內閣閣員與聯邦法院法官。***

* 美國總統大選是委任直選，而非公民直選，各州公民先選出該州的選舉人，再由選舉人代表該州投票。各州選民投票選出總統副總統，贏得一州多數普選票的候選人獲得該州全部選舉人票（採取「勝者全得制」），然後計算各州選舉人票之和，獲得半數以上選舉人票的候選人成為新任總統副總統。當初制憲人士不採普選而採選舉人團（Electoral College）制度，係為了保障各州權益，致有時產生候選人得到選民選票多，卻落選之情形。

** 英國內閣閣員須為國會二院之一的議員，表示向國會負責。反之美國行政機關乃單獨部門，獨立於立法機關之外，如議員充任閣員或其他行政職務，須辭去議員。且總統制之下，行政首長由選舉產生，有一定任期，僅對選民負責，不對國會負責。總統在職不依賴國會信任，即使不孚眾望，亦不能使其去職，不信任投票並不影響總統之職務。但行政部門所需經費有賴國會撥付。總統對閣員可任意任免，具有國家元首（比英國內閣總理有權）與行政首長雙重地位，閣員只是總統的機關，只對總統負責，不對國會負責，內閣會議決定只供總統參考。行政部門尚有獨立委員會（含州際商務委員會（ICC）、聯邦貿易委員會（FTC）等約10個）具有行政與司法權力，甚至立法權，可謂集三權於一身，號稱政府的第四部門。

*** 參院休會時，總統可臨時任命官員補缺，於開會時提請追認，稱為「休會任命」。

（五）Judicial Power 司法權

Federal judges are appointed by the President of the United States, and confirmed by a majority vote of the Senate. They see for life. The courts may declare laws unconstitutional. This rule of judicial review was established by John Marshall in Marburg v. Madison

(1803).The "supremacy" clause: the Constitution and federal laws take priority over state laws.*

　　聯邦法官由總統任命，參議院多數同意，爲終身職。法院可宣告法律違憲，此種司法審查之原則係由最高法院院長約翰馬歇爾在 Marburg 控 Madison（1803）一案所樹立（該院乃聯邦制度保障者與裁決者）。憲法定有「至高」條款：即憲法與聯邦法之效力優於各州之法律。

*1. 美國憲法第6條第2款規定有所謂至高條款（Supremacy Clause），明揭憲法、聯邦法律及美國對外條約爲「全國之最高法律」（the supreme law of the land），即美國法律體系的最高層次法律，位階高於各州的憲法與法律，即使牴觸州憲法與州法律，各州法官亦須加以捍衛。

 2. 美國司法系統二元化，聯邦法院與州法院並立。

 3. 憲法解釋權歸法院，「法官說什麼是憲法，什麼就是憲法」，所有憲法解釋都有政治上的影響。

 4. 美國與歐洲不同，並無特別憲法法院，各級法院都有司法審查權，即司法審查乃分散而非集中，而且法院於審理普通案件時，決定所生之憲法爭議。

（六）Divides Power between States and Federal Government 聯邦與各州政府分權

Powers not delegated to the United States* or denied to the states are reserved to the states. But the federal government has continuously expanded its power by means of "inter-state commerce" clause.

　　美國原採地方分權制，凡憲法未賦予聯邦或未否認各州之權力，保留予各州。但聯邦政府透過憲法上之州際通商條款**，不斷擴大其權力。

*馬歇爾院長在判例上樹立了：聯邦除憲法明示權力外，還有行使

此等權力所必需權力（默示權力）之原則。

**即〈規範與外國及州際及印第安部落通商〉條款（聯邦與各州權限劃分爭議，由司法部門尤其聯邦最高法院負責）。

（七）Full Faith and Credit 對他州之尊重

The "full faith and credit" clause requires that the legislative and judicial actions of one state be honored by the other states. A citizen of any state has the same privileges as citizens of all the other states.

「充分信任與尊重」條款要求各州之立法與司法行爲受到別州之尊重，任何州公民享有與所有他州公民相同之權利。*

*一州不得對非本州居民有歧視待遇。

（八）Rights of People 個人基本權利

Outlines many rights and freedoms of the people including freedom of religion, speech, press, assembly, the right to petition the government, no unreasonable searches or seizures, right to speedy, public, impartial trial by jury, right to bear arms, no excessive bail, no cruel and unusual punishment. Double jeopardy clause prevents a person from being tried twice for the same crime.

憲法揭示許多人民的權利與自由*，包括宗教、言論、出版、集會、向政府請願之權利、對犯罪被告無不合理搜索與扣押、保障由陪審團迅速、公開、公正審判、可攜帶武器**、無過重保釋金、禁止「殘酷與不尋常刑罰」，及犯罪一事不再理。

*定在1791年憲法之權利法案（章典）內。
**由於攜帶武器爲憲法所保障，致美國濫用槍枝危害治安之事件層出不窮。

（九）Expand to States 憲法影響各州

During subsequent decades, the Constitution abolished slave system. The Fourteenth Amendment forbad all states to deny to any person "life, liberty, or property" without due process of law and guarantee every person "the equal protection of its laws." Later it mandated women's suffrage; and granted suffrage to citizens 18 years of age and older etc., making the constitution's influence even more far-reaching.

於隨後幾十年間，憲法又修改，廢止奴隸制度，第十四修正條文*禁止各州未經「正當法律程序」，否認任何人之「生命、自由或財產」、保證所有人受到「法律平等保護」，後來又保護婦女參政權、賦予18歲以上公民參政權等，使憲法之影響更為深遠。

*權利章典最初係針對聯邦政府來保護人民，後來又透過憲法第十四修正條文擴張到限制各州對人民權利加以限制。

（十）Executive Orders 行政命令

The president can issue executive orders (including rules, regulations, and instructions) with legal effect binding upon federal agencies. They do not need approval of the Congress, but are subject to judicial review and interpretation.

總統可頒布對聯邦機構有法律拘束力之行政命令（包含規則、規章與指示），無需國會通過，但受司法審查與解釋。

（十一）President's Veto Power 總統之法案否決權

The U.S. president can veto any law passed by the Congress unless this veto is overridden by a 2/3 votes in both the Senate and the House.

美國總統可否決國會通過之法律，除非這項否決被參眾兩院以三分之二的票數駁回（總統及閣員無提案權）。

（十二）Expansion of Federal Power 聯邦權力之擴張

In addition to amending the constitution, Congress on innumerable occasions has given new scope to the constitution through statutes. The president also has used the executive agreement as an instrument of foreign policy.

除了修憲*外，國會不斷在許多場合透過制定法對憲法賦予新的意涵，總統亦經常利用行政協定作爲外交政策之工具，擴大聯邦政府之權力。

*也常透過最高法院的解釋，致聯邦權力不斷地擴張（尤其南北戰爭後）（聯邦有時對州有指導補助，現今各州對教育、衛生與福利管較多，又管銀行、保險、警察等）。

（十三）Political Questions 政治問題

The federal courts avoid to try political questions. They developed this doctrine as a means to avoid deciding some cases involving conflicts between the president and Congress.

聯邦法院避免審理政治問題（避免捲入政治漩渦），此原則之發展係爲了避免介入總統與國會衝突案件。*

*總統與國會間外交政策之爭議常認爲屬於政治問題。又法院只處理具體爭端，避免成爲行政或立法機關的顧問機關。

二、詞彙

due process of law：正當法律程序

the equal protection of its laws：法律之平等保護

framers：設計人、起草人

legislative, executive and judicial：立法、行政與司法

separation of powers：權力分立

the checks and balances：制衡

strike a balance：謀求平衡

main text comprises seven articles：主要原文有7條

vests：賦予

delegated to：授予

levy taxes：課稅

regulate interstate commerce：規範州際通商

declare war：宣戰

rules of procedure：程序規則

initiates impeachment proceedings：發動彈劾程序

senate adjudicates them：參議院審判他們

electoral college：選舉人團

chief executives：行政首長

commander in chief：統帥

concur：同意

granting pardons：准許赦免

vast appointment powers：巨大任命權

amendment：修正條文

vague：模糊

embrace：包括

final court of appeal：終審上訴法院

constitutionality：合憲

judicial review：司法審查

explicitly granted：明白賦予

principle of judicial review：司法審查原則

ruled：裁決

void national or state laws：全國或州法律無效

innumerable occasion：無數場合

territories：領土

succession：繼承

executive budget system：行政預算制度

the executive agreement：行政協定

custom and usage：慣例

presidential nomination procedures：總統提名程序

cabinet：內閣

convention：慣例

the full faith and credit clause：充分信任與尊重原則

immunities：免責

republican form of government：共和政體

stipulates：規定

convention：會議

ratified：批准

officeholders：公務員

public debts：公債

citing：引用

operational：生效

by implication：默示

enumerated：列舉的

residual：殘餘的

nullification：無效

racial segregation：種族隔離

regulatory power：規範之權力

preempted：排他的

writ of habeas corpus：人身保護令

bills of attainder and ex post facto laws：褫奪公權及溯及既往法律

the Bill of Rights：權利法案（章典）

rights of conscience：良心權

right of peaceful assembly and petition：和平集會與請願權利

unreasonable search and seizure：不合理搜查與扣押

self-incrimination：自證其罪

double jeopardy：一事不再理

excessive bail：過重保釋金

civil liberties：私人自由

to keep and bear arms：擁有與攜帶武器

assistance of counsel：律師協助

landmark decision：指標性判決

zoning laws：土地分區使用法

voting rights：投票權

gender discrimination：性別歧視

far-reaching：影響深遠的

mandated women's suffrage：強制婦女選舉權

shall not deprive any person of life, liberty, or property without due process of law：非經正當法律程序，不得剝奪生命、自由、財產

grant：賦予

public pressure：公共壓力

confirmed：同意、確認

salaries reduced：減俸

serve for life：終身職

the impeachment process：彈劾程序

the House of Representatives：眾議院

conviction：定罪

removed：免職

original jurisdiction：原始管轄權

geographically and subject matter based：基於地理與標的

intermediate appellate courts：中間上訴法院

appeals：上訴

trial courts：審判法院

discretionary：有裁量性

sit in panels of three judges：以三人之合議庭審理

subject-matter：標的

courts of general jurisdiction：有一般管轄權法院

federal question：聯邦問題

concurrent jurisdiction：競合管轄權

transferred, removed：移轉

stare decisis：遵循先例

writ of certiorari：准許向最高法院上訴令

discretionary：有裁量權

reverse, reversals：廢棄

statutory and constitutional issues：制定法與憲法爭議

criminal and most civil cases：刑事與大多民事案件

resolved：解決

legal motion or settlement：法律上聲請或和解

two levels of federal courts：兩級聯邦法院

the U.S. circuit courts of appeals：聯邦巡廻上訴法院

first instance：一審

a matter of right：有權

verdict：裁決

第二節　我國法

一、特色

1. According to Dr. Sun's Three Principles of the People, the government setup five powers of the government to create checks and balances, with examination and control powers deriving from executive and legislative powers on the one hand, and with political powers belonging to National Assembly on the other.

   依國父遺教（the Three Principles of the People，三民主義）五權分立，考試與監察二權自西方三權分出，政權機關有國民大會。

2. The central government and local government share their powers equally.

   中央與地方採均權主義。

3. The people have four political rights, namely: election, recall, initiative and referendum as well as freedom of speech, religion, writing, publication, and people of all races are treated equally.

   人民有選舉、罷免、創制、複決四種參政權，言論、信仰、著作、出版自由、各族平等。

4. The central government seems to adopt a hybrid system between both cabinet and presidential systems.

   中央政府似採內閣與總統折衷制。

5. The government enacted The Amendment of the Constitution to the constitution and abolished in 1991 the "Temporary Provisions Effective During the Period of Communist Rebellion".

   原有動員戡亂時期臨時條款，民國80年廢止臨時條款，制定憲法增修條文，修正條文中央採雙首長制。*

6. The Executive Yuan have several ministers without portfolio.

   行政院設有政務委員。

7. Unlike American system, the constitution is not interpreted by the Supreme Court, but is managed by Constitutional court consisting of all grand justices.

憲法不似美國由最高法院解釋，特設憲法法庭處理。

8. The judges decide cases independently.

法官獨立審判。

9. We do not adopt jury system.

不採陪審制。

10. The constitution has basic national policies provisions.

憲法列有基本國策。

*民國80年憲法增修條文內規定：「總統爲決定國家安全有關大政方針，得設國家安全會議及所屬國家安全局。」致國家安全會議成爲總統決定國家安全方針之諮詢機關。

二、詞彙

a democratic republic of the people：民主共和國

constitutional framework：憲政體制

republican system of government：共和政體

the sovereignty：主權

right of existence, work and property：生存權、工作權及財產權

freedom of residence and of change of residence：居住遷徙自由

freedom of speech：言論自由

freedom of correspondence：通訊自由

religious belief：宗教信仰

assembly and association：集會結社

writing and publication：寫作出版

the right of presenting petitions：請願

lodging complaints：訴願

instituting legal proceedings：提起訴訟

right of election, recall, initiative and referendum：選舉、罷免、創制、複決之權利

right of taking public examinations and of holding public offices：參加考試及服公職之權利

duty of performing military service：服兵役義務

ratified：批准

the Temporary Provisions：臨時條款

the state of emergency：緊急狀態

extra-constitutional powers：憲法以外權力

Three Principles of the People：三民主義（nationalism, democracy, and the livelihood of the people）

nationalism：民族主義

livelihood of the people：民生

a government of the people, by the people, and for the people：民有、民治、民享

National Assembly：國民大會

authoritative：權威的

commander-in-chief：統帥

concentrate：集中

a semi-presidential system：準總統制

separation of five powers：五權分立

the Executive Yuan：行政院

the Legislative Yuan：立法院

the Judicial Yuan：司法院

the Examination Yuan：考試院

the Control Yuan：監察院

legislative supremacy：立法優越（至上）

legacy：遺產

local autonomy：地方自治

inauguration：就職

supplemental elections：補選

transition to：過渡為

democratization：民主化

disbanded：解散

ratified by referendum：由複決承認

political consensus：政治上協議

quorum：同意票

preamble：前言

Chinese reunification：統一中國

issue emergency orders：發布緊急命令

command of the armed forces：統率三軍

promulgation of laws and decrees：公布法令

declaration of martial law with the approval of, or subject to confirmation by,
    the Legislative Yuan：經立法院同意或確認宣布戒嚴法

amnesties and pardons：大赦與特赦

remission of sentences：減刑

restitution of civil rights：復權

resolution：決議

report of state of the nation by the President：總統國情報告

no-confidence vote：不信任投票

dissolution of the Legislative Yuan：解散立法院

consulting with its president：諮詢該院長

cross-strait relations：海峽兩岸關係

advisory organization：諮詢機構

on the recommendation of the premier：經內閣總理推薦

Organic Act of the Executive Yuan：行政院組織法

Executive Yuan Council：行政院會議

commissions：委員會

entered into force：生效

renewable after re-election：連選可連任

Council of Grand Justices：大法官會議

power of judicial review：司法審查權

Public Prosecutor General：檢察總長

discipline of civil servants：公務員懲戒

adjudication of civil, criminal, and administrative litigations：審判民刑行政訴訟

unify the interpretation of laws and ordinances：統一法令解釋

the criminal justice system：刑事司法（訴訟）制度

shifted its operating method from ... to ...：其運作方法自⋯⋯變為⋯⋯

a judge-centred inquisitorial system：以法官為中心之糾問主義

an attorney-based adversarial system：以律師為中心之對立主義

the civil service：文官

better checks and balances：更佳制衡

consecutively：連續

qualification screening：銓敘

security of tenure：任期保障

pecuniary aid in case of death：撫卹

employment, discharge：任免

performance evaluations：考績

scale of salaries：級俸

promotions, transfers：升遷

commendations, rewards：褒獎

expiration of their original terms of office：原任期屆滿

impeachment：彈劾

censure：糾舉

audit：審計

Ministry of Audit：審計部

auditor-general：審計長

final accounts of revenues and expenditures：收支之決算

line of demarcation：分界線

nature of business：事務之性質

pertains to：涉及

self-government：自治

Special Municipality：直轄市

mayors：市長

county councils：縣議會

considerable degree of autonomy to local governments：地方政府相當程度自治

martial law was lifted：解除戒嚴法

undergone seven rounds of revision：經7次修改

accountable：負責

access to：獲取

undergoing restructuring：改造中

returned to power：重新執政

democratization：民主化

第三節　習題

選擇題（四選一）

1. The president of the U.S. can be impeached by _____.

  (1) senate

  (2) house of representative

  (3) congress

  (4) chief of justice of the Supreme Court

2. The federal courts avoid to try _____. They developed this doctrine as a means to avoid deciding some cases involving conflicts between the president and Congress.

(1) philosophical questions

(2) political questions

(3) economic questions

(4) academic questions

3. The federal government has continuously increased its power through _____.

(1) equal protection clause

(2) full faith and credit clause

(3) interstate clause

(4) due press clause

4. The president used to make _____ with foreign countries.

(1) diplomatic agreements

(2) executive agreements

(3) treaties

(4) laws

5. The president can not grant pardon to _____?

(1) his family

(2) any traitor

(3) himself

(4) his opponent

6. The number of senator for each state is _____ persons.

(1) 2

(2) 3

(3) 4

(4) according to the population of each state

7. There are _____ justices in the U.S. Supreme Court.
   (1) 5
   (2) 7
   (3) 9
   (4) 8

8. At present in U.S., anybody who is _____ years old has right to vote.
   (1) 20
   (2) 18
   (3) 21
   (4) 19

9. The U.S. president can veto any law passed by the Congress unless this veto is overridden by a _____ votes in both the Senate and the House.
   (1) half
   (2) more than half
   (3) unanimous
   (4) 2/3

10. In U.S., federal courts exercise _____ jurisdiction over crimes & civil cases than state courts.
    (1) more
    (2) less
    (3) about the same
    (4) depends on different year

11. The people's rights protected by U.S. Constitution was also applicable to state courts _____.
    (1) from its enactment.
    (2) after Second World War
    (3) after the civil war
    (4) after First World War

12. The misuse of gun by people in U.S. is attributed to the right of ___
    ____.
    (1) jury system
    (2) carrying fire arms
    (3) no excessive bail
    (4) no cruel penalty
13. According to U.S. Constitution, federal government has _____
    __ power as (than) state government because states have residual
    powers.
    (1) same
    (2) more
    (3) about the same
    (4) less
14. In U.S., the time women started to vote was _____.
    (1) since independence
    (2) after civil war
    (3) after First World War
    (4) after constitution came into effect
15. Under U.S. constitution, jury trial are protected in _____ cases.
    (1) both civil and criminal
    (2) only criminal
    (3) civil
    (4) none
16. The U.S. president's term of office is _____.
    (1) 2 terms
    (2) 3 terms
    (3) only one term
    (4) two and half

17. Originated from England, _____ is also protected under U.S. constitution.
    (1) right of carry weapon
    (2) right of voting
    (3) right of religion
    (4) right of habeas corpus

18. In order to manage the government, the U.S. president may issue rules, regulations, and instructions called _____. They have the legal effect binding upon federal agencies but do not need approval of the Congress.
    (1) proclamations
    (2) executive orders
    (3) decrees
    (4) mandamus

▲選擇題解答

1. (2)　2. (2)　3. (3)　4. (2)　5. (3)　6. (1)　7. (3)　8. (2)　9. (4)

10. (2)　11. (3)　12. (2)　13. (4)　14. (2)　15. (1)　16. (1)　17. (4)　18. (2)

第四節　詞彙整理

一、同義詞

grant－vest

二、反義詞

implied; express

territory; exteriority; extraterritoriality

三、詞性轉換

（一）動詞 → 名詞

command → commander, commandment

ratify → ratification

acquire → acquisition

impeach → impeachment

constitute → constitution

depose → depositions

tax → taxation

divide → division

rule → regulation

consent → consensus

prevent → prevention

elect → election

declare → declaration

extradite → extradition

deport → deportation

stipulate → stipulation

amend → amendment

prevent → prevention

abolish → abolishment

forbid → forbiddance

deny → denial

guarantee → guaranty

require → requirement

expand → expansion

delegate → delegation

secure → security

separate → separation

execute → execution

（二）名詞 → 形容詞

pardon → pardonable

legislation → legislative

justice → judicial

constitution → constitutional

charge → chargeable

faith → faithful

excess → excessive

prevention → preventive

commerce → commercial

influence → influential

honor → honorable

power → powerful

emergency → emergent

aggression → aggressive

speed → speedy

execution → executive

（三）形容詞 → 名詞

cruel → cruelty

free → freedom

equal → equality

impartial → impartiality

subsequent → subsequence

supreme → supremacy

（四）動詞或名詞 → 身分類名詞

command → commander

senate → senator

legislate → legislator

represent → representative

第二章　　契約法

第一節　美國法

一、緒言

In US law, they do not have concept of law of obligations, neither do they have general part as we. Contract is the most basic subject of law and important course in law school. Contract law covers capacity, form, offer and acceptance, consideration, fraud, mistake, interpretation, performance, conditions, rights of assignee, third party beneficiary, and remedies. It approximately covers most parts of our law of general part of civil law and of law of obligations. Apart from certain exceptions, it also applies to other areas such as lease, employment, sale of goods, real estate and insurance, etc.

　　美國法並無大陸法債法之觀念，也缺少總則觀念。美國契約法是美國最基本法律與法律學院課目之一，涵蓋契約之能力、形式、要約、承諾、約因、詐欺、錯誤合法性、解釋、履行、履行之條件、受讓人之權利、債之消滅、第三人利益契約之受益人及救濟。相當於我們民總與債總的大部。契約法之原則除了若干例外外，也適用於諸如租賃、僱傭、買賣物品或土地、保險等不同領域之約定。*

*Farnsworth, An Introduction to the Legal System of the United States, (1975 ed.) 119-120.

In addition to common law, chapter 1, 2 and 9 of Uniform Commercial Code as well as states' consumer protection law (statutes) regulate contractual relations, therefore contracts are very complicated. Besides the role of statutes becomes more and more important. However there are still no federal uniform contract law so far. Not every contract applies contract law.

契約法的法源除普通法（判例法）外，還有統一商法典（Uniform Commercial Code）第一章總則、第二章買賣及第九章擔保交易以及聯邦與各州的消費者保護法，也對契約加以規範。換言之，契約法除了普通法（含衡平法）外，還包含制定法（包括聯邦與各州之各種消費者保護法，統一商法典等），即除普通法外，更混合了州法與聯邦法及統一法等，異常複雜，而且制定法的角色愈來愈重要，惟至今尚無聯邦統一契約法。同時，各種契約並非都適用契約法，而且有關規定還分散各處。

二、美國契約法之特色

1. Consideration is a special feature of Anglo-American contract law. But its importance has decreased.
   契約須有約因，即約因是英美契約法之特色，為大陸法系民法所無，惟已式微。

2. In US, an acceptance not by dialogue between two parties becomes effective at the moment of dispatch, rather than reaching/the other party as our law.
   美國法下非對話意思表示之情形，承諾之效力採發信主義，而非我國民法之到達主義。

3. There are only two kinds of legal capacity, those who have and those who have not. They do not have restrictive legal capacity like our law.
   美國法下人之行為能力只分有與無兩種，而無我國限制行為能力這一級。

4. Gift contract usually cannot be enforced.
   贈與契約在美國法上通常不能執行。

5. There are different kinds of estoppels in order to prevent the debtor from damaging the other party. It seems they are more concrete and concise than our principle of honesty and good faith.
   有各種禁反言制度（詳後）防止損害相對人，比大陸法誠實信用原則似更具體明確。

6. American law has Enforceable and Unenforceable contracts.
   美國契約有可執行與不可執行之契約之分類。

7. Injunction may also order the debtor to do an affirmative act.
   禁制令是命被告從事或停止為特定行為，故其內容並不以禁止被告之積極行為為限，也有命義務人為積極行為。

8. Specific performance are only granted in case monetary compensation is not adequate remedy for the creditor. But there are no such limit in our law.
   在債務人不履行時，以不能由金錢賠償獲得滿足之情形為限，債權人才能請求法院對債務人強制執行（specific performance，特定履行）但我強制執行法並無此限制。

9. Undue influence, misrepresentation and economic duress may be used as a ground for cancelling a contract. This is more lenient than our law.
   不正影響、不正表述與經濟上脅迫亦可作為撤銷契約之原因，比我民法規定為寬。

10. Sometimes the judge may order the debtor by contempt of court to pay. But under our law the judge cannot do so.
    有時法官可以蔑視法庭之理由命債務人履行，但我法律下法官無此權力。

11. Different from our law, in a breach of contract, the victim owes a duty of mitigating the damages.

　　債務人不履行時，被害人負減輕損失義務，而我民法則無此義務。

12. In order to avoid unjust enrichment, a court often implies the existence of a contract.

　　為了避免不當得利，法院常默示有契約存在。

13. The US has a parol evidence rule.

　　美國有特殊之口頭證據法則（詳後）。

14. Frustration of purpose may also void the contracts.

　　契約目的不能達到，亦係契約消滅之原因。

15. There are no uniform rules for statute of limitation.

　　消滅時效缺乏統一規定。

16. Statute's wording is rather long. Mutates mutandis seldom appears.

　　制定法規定之語句較為冗長，很少準用或類推適用之規定。

17. Government contract is very well developed.

　　政府契約（例如政府採購等）另成為一個特殊領域，特別發達。

三、介紹

　　Contracts are agreements between private parties creating mutual obligations enforceable by law. Their basic elements are: mutual assent; expressed by offer and acceptance; consideration; capacity; and legality.

　　契約是私人間產生法律上可執行之相互義務之約定。其基本要素是相互同意（要約與承諾）、約因、行為能力及合法性。

（一）Types of Contract 契約之種類

1. Express Contract and Implied Contract 明示契約與默示契約

(1) Express Contract 明示契約

The promises are communicated by language, either oral or written.

由語言（口頭或書面）所作之允諾。

(2) Implied Contract 默示契約

The conduct of the parties indicates that they consented to be bound.

由當事人之行為顯示其同意受契約之拘束。

2. Unilateral Contract and Bilateral Contract 單務契約與雙務契約

(1) Unilateral Contract 單務契約

A person accepts an offer by performing a requested act. The terms of the offer must clearly indicate that an act is required for acceptance.

對要約之承諾須履行要約人所要求之行為。要約之內容須明白表示承諾須以某行為為之。

(2) Bilateral Contract 雙務契約

A person accepts an offer by promising to do the requested act.

一方以允諾作對方要求之行為來接受要約。

3. Conditional Contracts (condition precedent & condition subsequent) 附條件契約

Conditional contracts are effective or terminated upon the completion of a specific event. A condition precedent means the occurrence of fact, at the date of the agreement, is uncertain and the condition must occur before duty of performance arises in the other party. A condition subsequent is one that cuts off an already existing duty of performance and brings the obligation to an end.

附條件契約係指契約於訂約時是否發生某事實（條件），並不確定，如一旦發生時，契約始生效力者，稱為附停止條件；如契約已生效力，而於日後某事實一旦發生時，契約效力歸於消滅者，則稱為附解除條件。*

＊基本上與我民法上之附停止與附解除條件相當。

4. Adhesion Contract 附合契約

Adhesion contracts are those giving one party unequal bargaining power, or being unfair and unconscionable resulting in a "take it or leave it" situation; e.g., mortgage agreements, lease agreements, online purchase etc. The court often pays attention to them and tries to protect the consumers.

附合契約係指契約予一方，比另一方不公平之折衝能力，或因不公平與不合情理，致形成「要或拉倒」之情形，例如抵押契約，租賃契約，線上買賣契約等，法院往往對這種契約特別注意，以保護消費者。*

＊或稱定型化契約（standard form contracts）。

5. Enforceable and Unenforceable 可執行與不可執行之契約

An enforceable contract means the court will compel a party to perform or compensate the other for not fulfilling the contract terms.

An unenforceable contract means the court will not compel a party to perform or compensate the other for not fulfilling the contract terms.

可執行契約係指法院會命當事人履行義務或賠償他方不履行義務之契約；而不可執行之契約係指法院無法強制當事人履行或賠償他方不履行義務之契約。

（二）Capacity to Make Juridical Acts 從事法律行爲之能力

Legal Capacity 行爲能力

Legal capacity is what a human being can do within the framework of the legal system including: making a binding legal agreement, suing another person and making other decisions of a legal nature.

行爲能力係指人在法制範圍內作爲之能力，包括締結有效契約、控告他人及作其他法律性質決定之能力。*

*美國法下行爲能力只分有與無，而無我國限制行爲能力這一級。

Minors (individuals under age 18) and people who are mentally incompetent do not have the legal capacity to enter into contracts.

未成年人（18歲以下）與精神不健全之人無締結契約之行爲能力。

A contract between a minor and an adult is binding on the adult but may be cancelled upon request of the minor at any time during minority or within a reasonable time after majority except contracts for necessaries.

未成年人與成人間之契約，拘束該成年人，但除生活必需品契約外，可由未成年人在未成年期間或成年後之合理期間內取消。*

*此點與我民法不同，對未成年人固屬優厚，然對相對人不免過苛。我國民法第79條規定限制行爲能力人未得法定代理人之允許，所訂立之契約，須經法定代理人之承認，始生效力。若經承認則有效、拒絕就無效。相對人可定一個月以上之期限，催告未成年人之法定代理人，確答是否承認。

The test for mental capacity to enter into a contract is whether the person had the ability to understand the nature and consequences of the agreement.

有無締約之精神能力，視行爲人能否了解契約之性質與效果而定。

Corporations have the power to enter into contracts through the acts of their agents, officers and authorized employees.

公司可透過其代理人、職員及被授權之受雇人與他人締約。

（三）Elements of a Contract 契約之要素

1. Offer 要約

One of the parties made a promise to do or refrain from doing some specified action in the future.

指當事人之一方他日作某種行爲或不爲一定行爲之允諾。

2. Consideration 約因

Consideration is a feature of Anglo-American contract law. Consideration is a promise, an act, or a promise not to act. Something of value (money, service or not to do something.) was promised in exchange for the specified action or nonaction. The most common form is paying money. Consideration can not be something you provided in the past. As long as the consideration is not sham or token, it needs not be fair or adequate. In some states, consideration can be satisfied by a valid substitute.

約因是英美契約法之特色。約因是一種允諾、一種行爲或一種不作爲之允諾。允諾是以有價值的金錢、服務或不作爲，以交換特定之行爲或不行爲。最常見的形態是給付金錢。約因須係現實的*，過去提供之約因尚屬不足。惟約因只要不是虛假或象徵性，無需充分或公平。有一些州可以有效的其他方法滿足約因之要求。**

*贈與契約在美國法上通常不能訴請法院執行（promise to make a gift is usually unenforceable），因認爲此種允諾並無約因，此點亦與我國法不同。

**晚近美國法下約因制度已經式微或放寬。

3. Acceptance 承諾

The offer was accepted unambiguously. Acceptance may be expressed through words, deeds or performance as called for in the contract. Generally, the acceptance must mirror the terms of the offer. If not, the acceptance is viewed as a rejection and counter offer.

對要約之承諾須明確。承諾可以言詞、行為或契約所定之履行行為加以表示。通常承諾須與要約之內容相同，否則會被視為拒絕與反對要約。*

* 美國法上非對話意思表示之效力係採發信主義，而非我民法之到達主義。

4. Mutuality 相互

The contracting parties had "a meeting of the minds" regarding the agreement. This means the parties understood and agreed to the basic substance and terms of the contract.

契約當事人對契約須有「意思合致」，即雙方了解與同意契約之基本實質內容。

5. Invitation 要約引誘

An invitation to treat is not a contract. For an invitation to treat (e.g., advertisement) is only inviting the other party to make an offer.

要約之引誘並非契約，因要約之引誘（如廣告）只是邀他方作要約而已。

（四）Is a Contract Must be in Writting? 契約有訂立書面之必要？

In general, a contract needs not be in writing. But the Statute of Frauds requires certain types of contracts to be in writing, such as those over $500, marriage contracts, contracts not to be performed within one year, interest in land contracts.

　　契約原則上不必訂立書面，但詐欺防止法（Statute of Frauds）*
要求某些／種契約作成書面，例如超過500美元之契約、結婚契
約、一年後履行之契約，及不動產契約須作成書面契約。**

* 詐欺防止法爲繼受自英國之制定法

** 美國又有特殊之口頭證據法則（parol evidence rule），規定如契
　約當事人已將契約訂了書面，且意欲以其作爲完全且最後之約
　定者（例如契約內有 merger clause△，該書面就成爲該交易之完
　全紀錄，當事人日後不得另提證據證明契約另有約定或已有所
　改變，此原則對消費者可能構成陷阱。

　△即訂有一切磋商約定已併入該合約之條款。

（五）Vitiating Factors Make a Contract Void or Voidable 契約無效或撤銷之原因

After a contract becomes effective, both parties are obligated to
perform their duties. However, in the following situations a contract
may become invalid or may be rescinded by the other party.

　　契約生效後雙方負履行義務，但有下列情況時，契約可能歸於
無效或由他方撤銷：

1. Against Public Policy 違反公序良俗*

* 英美法上公序良俗，稱爲 public policy。

2. Impossibility or Frustration of Purpose 客觀不能或契約目的不能達到

If a later and unforeseen event makes performance of the contract
objectively impossible (impossibility) or make a party's purpose for
entering into the contract frustrated, of which the other party knew
at the time of entering the contract (frustration or impracticability of
purpose), a party's contract performance may be excused. E.g., after a

construction contracts was signed and the building itself was destroyed before the performance is due.

　　契約生效後，由於嗣後發生不可預見之事故，致履行變成客觀不能或一方之契約目的不能達到（他方於訂約時所知），例如承攬契約訂立後於履行期前，建物本身已焚毀者，則可免一方之履行義務。

3. Act of God, Force Majeure 不可抗力

An act of God means an event beyond human control or activity, such as a natural disaster like flood or earthquake.

　　不可抗力係指發生洪水或地震之類自然災變，非人力所能控制之事故。

4. Illegal 契約不法

Illegal subject matter or illegal means of performance.
包括標的不法或履行方式不法。

5. Mistake 錯誤

When consent to a contract is gained due to a bilateral mistake of fact, the contract is said to be void but when the mistake occurs due to a unilateral mistake of fact, the agreement is valid except in the cases of mistake regarding the nature of the contract or identity of the parties to the contract.

　　契約之同意，出於雙方對事實之錯誤時，契約無效。但由於一方對事實之錯誤時，除對契約之性質或當事人同一性有錯誤外，契約仍屬有效。

6. Mentally Incompetent 心智不健全

One or both parties lack legal capacity, such as sixteen years old or mentally incompetent.

　　當事人一方或雙方欠缺行為能力，例如一方才16歲或精神欠健全。

7. Fraud and Misrepresentation 詐欺與不正表述

A false statement or information that induces one party to enter into a contract with another. The aggrieved party can claim compensation for that loss if he shows that: he was misled and relied upon that false information when entering into the contract.

指一方用不實陳述或資訊，引誘他方締結契約。被害人如能證明被誤導，且締約時係信賴該錯誤資訊時，可請求賠償損失。

8. Duress or Undue Influence 脅迫或不正影響

Duress can be committed by violence, imprisonments or threat of those act. Undue influence means someone takes advantage of the party's vulnerability to pressure.

脅迫可出於暴力、囚禁或威脅等行為，而不正影響係指一方利用他方易受壓力之影響而得利。

9. Economic Duress 經濟上脅迫

When unfair and extreme commercial pressure is applied to a party to enter a contract or vary an existing contract, the contract may be declared void.

用不公平與極端之商業上壓力，使一方締結契約或改變現存契約者，該契約可歸於無效。*

*此點比我國民法規定寬鬆，對弱者較為優厚。

10. Unconscionability 不道德

It means a contract is particularly harsh or oppressive. One party has almost no choice but to agree to the terms of the agreement. This often occurs in standardized contract case.

指契約非常苛酷或不公，一方須接受契約內容，幾無選擇餘地。常在定型化契約案件發生。*

* 如與我國法比較，美國法下，違約之一方可主張之抗辯種類甚多，包括不正表述、不正影響、經濟上脅迫，甚至不道德亦可構成契約得撤銷之原因，範圍比我國民法爲廣，尤其多出一個影響契約效力之不正影響。

（六）Third-Party Beneficiary Contract 第三人利益契約

A third-party beneficiary may legally enforce that contract, but only after his or her rights have already been vested (either by the contracting parties' assent or by justifiable reliance on the promise).

第三人利益契約之第三人在其權利由於契約當事人同意，或合理信賴該允諾而確定時，始可在法律上請求債務人履行。

1. Assignment 債權讓與

All contractual rights may be assigned, except:

(1) substantially change the debtor's duty or risk.

(2) prohibited by law.

所有契約上權利除下列情形外，均可讓與：

(1) 實質改變債務人義務或風險者。

(2) 法律禁止者。

2. Novation 契約權利與義務同時讓與

It means to substitute a new party for an original party to the contract. It requires assent of all parties and completely releases the original party.

指以一新當事人取代契約原當事人，此人須全體當事人同意後，完全免除原當事人責任。

3. Duty to Perform Becomes Discharged 履行義務之消滅

Grounds for discharging duty of performance:

(1) performance: the parties are discharged from the contract, and the contract is terminated.

(2) occurrence of condition subsequent.

(3) novation.

(4) assignment.

(5) accord and satisfaction.

(6) release.

(7) rescission.

(8) modification of contract.

(9) substituted contract.

(10) running of statute of limitations.

履行義務消滅之原因：

(1)契約因當事人履行而終止。

(2)解除條件成就。

(3)契約權利與義務同時讓與。

(4)契約權利之讓與。

(5)代物清償當事人接受代替性之履行。

(6)免除。

(7)解除。

(8)修改契約。

(9)代替契約。

(10) 時效完成。

（七）Breach of Contract 契約不履行

Kinds of breach of contract:
債務不履行的種類：

1. Actual Breach 真正不履行

When the parties specifically provides that "time is of the essence" (i.e. deadlines are firm), failure to perform at the agreed time will constitute an actual breach. The non-breaching party can terminate the contract.

如雙方特別規定履行之「期限重要」（例如截止日確定），而一方未於約定期間履行時，成立真正違約，未違約之一方可終止契約。

2. Anticipatory Breach 預期不履行

When one party indicates (notice) unwillingness or inability to perform obligations under the contract, the non-breaching party can terminate the contract.

一方（於履行期前）向對方預先表示（通知）不願或不能履行時，未違約之他方可終止契約。

3. Minor Breach 輕微不履行

When a party fails to perform some part of his obligation. Since the entire contract has not been breached, the non-breaching party may only be able to pursue a remedy for financial loss resulted.

如一方僅部分違約，由於非全部違約，未違約之一方只能要求賠償違約之經濟上損失。*

*即此時未違約之一方仍須履行契約義務。

（八）Remedies for Breach Contract 不履行之救濟

1. Types of Remedies 救濟之種類

Remedies include award of damage, rescission and restitution. Sometimes count may order special performance or injunction.

救濟包括賠償損害、解除與回復原狀。有些情況法院會下特定履行令或禁制令。

(1) Award of Damages 損害賠償

(2) Injunction 禁制令

An injunction is a court order requiring the defendant to do (mandatory injunction) or cease doing a specific action (negative injunction).There are three types of injunctions: Permanent Injunctions, Temporary Restraining Orders and Preliminary Injunctions.

禁制令是命被告從事（強制禁制令）或停止為特定行為（消極禁制令）。禁制令有三種：永久禁制令、暫時禁制令及初期禁制令。

(3) Specific Performance 特定履行

Specific performance is usually ordered in cases wherein an award of damages would not be enough to remedy the situation, such as delivery of a piece of land.

如金錢賠償損害不足以救濟原告之損害時，法院可命被告履行特定之行為，例如交付買賣約定移轉之土地（營造契約、個人服務）。

(4) Restitution 回復原狀

Restoration to the former or original state or position, such as restoration of something to its rightful owner, or making good of or giving an equivalent for some injury.

恢復至以前或原來之狀態，諸如將物歸還原主或補償損失或給付相同之物。

(5) Rescission 解除

Canceling a contract and eliminate all its effects and put the parties back to their original position before the agreement was made.

撤銷原契約，消除契約所有效力，使當事人恢復契約訂立前的狀態。

2. Types of Damages 損害賠償之種類*

*當事人可在契約上訂立違約金條款以免證明損害之煩。

(1) Compensatory Damages 補償性損害賠償

Also called "actual damages". But the amount should reduce those which the victim could reasonably avoided or substantially ameliorated for the victim owes duty to mitigate the loss pursuant American law.

亦稱為真正損害，旨在補償債權人之損失。惟因債權人對債務人之債務不履行，負減輕損失之義務，故實際賠償額中可能要扣除債權人可合理避免損失之數額，而不能請求因違約所致之全額損失。此點與我國民法不同。又分為下列兩種：

① General Damages 一般損害

They refer to direct and necessary damages resulting from the breach.

指因違約直接與必然蒙受之損失，為最常見之損害。

② Special Damages 特別損害

Also called "consequential damages". They refer special circumstances or conditions that are not ordinarily predictable. The victim should prove that at the time the contract was signed the defendant knew or should have known his special needs or circumstances.

亦稱為「consequential damages」，指通常無法預期之特殊情形所受之損害。是真正損失，但非直接與立即方式，未違反之一方須證明於訂約時明知或知悉特殊情形或需要。

(2) Punitive Damages 懲罰性損害賠償

Punitive Damages which are also called "exemplary damages" are awarded to punish a wrongdoer acted willfully, maliciously or fraudulently. It may awarded together with compensatory damages. The court often award such damages in tort cases, but not in contract cases.

至於懲罰性損害賠償亦稱為「exemplary damages」。法院很少在違約場合判給此種賠償，而常在侵權行為判給。它是用以懲罰故意、惡意或詐欺之侵權人，可與補償性損害賠償一併請求。

（九）Sale 買賣

The Uniform Commercial Code has special provisions for sales including sale on approval, auction, installment contract, allocation of interest and risk of loss, passage of title, right to cure, right of rejection, replevy, Bailee, etc.

UCC（統一商法典）對買賣另有規定，包含試驗買賣、拍賣、分期付款契約、利益分配與損失分擔、權利移轉、治癒權、拒絕權、取回權（＝replevin取回物，乃一種物上請求權）、受寄人等。

對於不負瑕疵擔保責任之聲明（disclaimer of warranty），該法典定有：

1. Express Warranty 明示擔保責任
2. Implied Warranty 默示擔保責任

又分為：

(1) warranty of title (good title, no lien or encumbrances).

(2) warranty of merchantability (fit for ordinary purposes).

(1) 權利瑕疵擔保責任（權利無瑕疵，無留置權或負擔）。

(2) 即商品適合出售（適於該商品的通常用途）。*

* 與我民法物的瑕疵擔保責任相似。

（十）Sale of Consumer's Goods 消費者買賣部分

Their intents include door-to-door sale, pyramid schemes, agency, principal and agent, etc.

內容涉及挨戶推銷、老鼠會、代理、本人與代理人等。

（十一）Others 其他

1. Equitable Doctrine of Promissory Estoppel 禁反言之法理與原則

If one party has made reasonable reliance to his detriment on the assurances/promises of the other party, the court may award the non-breaching party a reliance damages to compensate the party for the amount suffered as a result of the party's reasonable reliance on the agreement.

因他方擔保或允諾，致一方受損失時，法院可能命他方賠償未違約之一方因合理信賴約定所受的信賴損失。

2. Quasi-Contract (Unjust Enrichment) 準契約*（不當得利）

The court may award unjust enrichment to a party, if the party who confers a benefit on another party, if it would be unjust for the party receiving the benefit to keep it without paying for it.

如受領一方之受益不合理，法院可能賦予他方不當得利之救濟。

*準契約並非美國法上的契約，但基於公平之見地，對受損人賦予此種救濟。我國民法則定為不當得利。又美國法似無因管理之規定。

3. Fraudulent Transfer 詐害性移轉

Those acts which are called fraudulent transfer (approximately similar to our Civil Code article 244) may be rescinded by the creditors.

詐害債權人之行為（相當我民法244條）稱為詐害性移轉，債權人可撤銷之。

4. Contract Clause 契約條款

In practice American contract are often very detailed and complex. They tend to be adhesion contracts or standard form contracts. If their clauses can be separated, they are called having severability. Practical contracts include applicable law, liquidated damages, arbitration, surety, joint and severally liability, indemnification clause, etc.

美國實務上契約條款往往訂得非常詳盡且複雜，且多屬定型化契約，其內容如可分割，稱為有分割性。實際契約往往定有準據法（applicable law）、違約金、仲裁、保證人、連帶負責、補償條款等條款。

5. Consumer Protection Lan 消費者保護法

US has consumer protection law which influenced our law.
美國另有保護消費者的法律，影響我國立法。

6. Anti-trust Law 反壟斷法

US has antitrust law which influenced many countries including ours.

美國有禁止獨占及不正競業的法律，影響大陸法系國家，包含我國的公平交易法。

7. Trust Law 信託法

US has trust law which influenced many countries including ours.
英美有信託法，影響不少大陸法系，包含我國的信託法。

（注）本文參考

1. Contract Law Tutorial for Judges in New Mexico
   http://jec. unm.edu/education/online-training/contract-law-tutorial/ introduction
2. https://www.law.cornell.edu/wex/contract
3. ABA, You and the Law (Publications International, Ltd.,1990).
4. 楊崇森，美國契約法之理論與運用，專法專刊，60卷5期（民國103年10月），頁55-78；61卷6期（民國104年1月），頁56-80。

四、詞彙

Restatement：整編

executed contract：已執行契約

executory contract：待執行契約

void contract：無效契約

voidable contract：得撤銷契約

enforceable contract：可執行契約

unenforceable contract：不可執行契約

express contract：明示契約

implied contract：默示契約

minor：未成年人

juridical acts：法律行為

juridical person：法人

against public policy or morals：違反公序良俗

consideration：約因

bargain：討價還價

predictable：可預測的

promisor：允諾人

promisee：被允諾人

Statute of Frauds：禁止詐欺條例

UCC：統一商法典

construe：解釋

revoke：取消

reject：拒絕

assignment：讓與

notarize：公證

risk of loss：危險負擔

failure to deliver：怠於交付

deposit：擔保金

parole evidence rule：口頭證據法則

waiver：棄權

merger：合併

integration clause：併入條款

surety：保證人

guarantor：擔保人

trade practices：貿易習慣

invitation to treat：要約之引誘

legal remedy：法律上救濟

force majeure：不可抗力

good faith：善意

standard form contract：定型化契約

acknowledge：承認

merit：值得

contingency：變數、未定

condition：條件

condition precedent：停止條件

condition consequent：解除條件

excuse：免責原因

duress：脅迫

mistake：錯誤

mutual mistake：相互錯誤

common mistake：共同錯誤

unilateral mistake：單方錯誤

intermediary：傳達人

transmission：傳達

undue influence：不正影響

fraud：詐欺

misrepresentation：不正表述

unconscionable：無道德

exculpatory clause：排除條款

public policy：公序良俗

promissory estoppel：允諾禁反言

form book：格式大全

contract of adhesion：附合契約

offer：要約

acceptance：承諾

promise：允諾

invitation for offer：要約之引誘

counter offer：反要約

gentlemen's agreement：君子協定

domestic agreement a：家內契約

social agreement ：社會契約

commercial agreement ：商業契約

letter of intent：意向書

memorandum of understanding：備忘錄

withdraw：撤回

terminated：終止

rescission：解除

modification：更改

composition agreement：和解契約

restrictive convenant：限制使用契約

agency contract：代理契約

principal：本人

apparent authority：表見授權

power of attorney：授權書

lease：租賃

partnership：合夥契約

limited partnership：有限合夥

general partnership：一般合夥

negotiable instrument ：流通證券

warranty：擔保

express warranty：明示擔保

implied warranty of merchantability：適於買賣之默示擔保

warranty of title：權利瑕疵擔保

sales by description or sample：描述買賣或貨樣買賣

label：標籤

disclaim：不擔保

disclaimer：不擔保之聲明

clear title：權利無瑕疵

warranty of fitness for a particular purpose：適於特定目的之擔保

indemnify：補償

pledge：質權

chattel mortgage：動產抵押

conditional sale：附條件買賣

collateral：擔保

financial statement：財務報告

inventory：財產清單

seize(v.) / seizure(n.)：扣押

self - help repossession：自力取回

fraudulent transfer：詐欺移轉

ordinary course of business：通常商業過程

government contract：政府契約

default clause：不履行（遲延）條款

franchise agreement：授權契約

claim：請求

estoppel：禁反言

equitable estoppel：衡平法上禁反言

doctrine of substantial performance：實質履行原則

good faith：善意

rescind：撤銷、解除

repudiation：拒絕履行契約

impossibility：不能

impracticability：不可行

frustration of purpose：目的無法達成

reformation：修改契約

breach：不履行

material breach：重大不履行

minor breach：輕微不履行

expectation damages：期待損害賠償

mitigation of damages：減少損失

foreseeability：可預見

liquidated damages：違約金

specific performance：特定履行

restitution：回復原狀

quasi-contract：準契約，不當得利

third party beneficiary：第三受益人

joint and several liability：連帶責任

discharge of contract：契約之消滅

performance：履行

accord and satisfaction：代物清償

assignment：移轉

novation：更改

delegation：授權

release：放棄

contract not to sue：不告人契約

specific performance 特定履行

Conditional contracts：附條件契約

Joint and several contracts：多數當事人契約

bargaining power：磋商（交涉）能力

第二節　我國法

一、特色

1. Consideration is not recognized in our law.
   契約不須有約因。
2. Gift contract is a valid contract.
   贈與契約有效。
3. An expression of communication between two persons not by dialogue becomes effective upon receipt by the other party.
   非對話意思表示於到達相對人時生效。
4. Undue influence, undue representation as well as economical duress are not grounds for cancelling contracts.
   不正影響與不正表述與經濟上脅迫似難作爲撤銷契約之原因。
5. We have provisions governing unjust enrichment and manage other's business without authorization.
   有不當得利與無因管理。
6. As a rule our judges can not compel a debtor to pay by citing contempt of court.
   法官一般難以蔑視法庭之理由命債務人履行（強制執行法有時可能）。
7. Under our Compulsory Execution Law the personal execution is also available, in addition to monetary compensation.
   特定履行在我強制執行法並無限於不能金錢賠償之限制。
8. We do not have estoppel system.
   無禁反言制度。

9. As for legal capacity, we have also a class of restrictive capacity.
行為能力方面，我國有限制行為能力這一級。

10. We have provisions governing standardized Statute of Limitation.
消滅時效有統一規定。

11. In breach of contract case, the creditor does not have the duty to mitigate his damages.
債務人不履行時，被害人不負減輕損失義務。

12. We do not have parole evidence rule.
無口頭證據法則。

13. The wording of legal provisions are concise.
法條文字簡潔。

二、詞彙

expression of intent：意思表示

unconsciousness or mental disorder：無意識或心神喪失

void：無效

valid：有效

unilateral act：單獨行為、單方行為

approval of his guardian：監護人之同意

withdraw：撤回

pure acquisition of a legal advantage：純獲法律上利益

acknowledgement of the guardian：監護人之承認

mutatis mutandis applied：準用

agent：代理人

principal：本人

scope of his delegated power：授權範圍內

takes effect directly：立即生效

mutatis mutandis applied：準用之

rather than：而非……

literal meaning of the words：文字之表面意義

expresser：表意人

limitations or other alterations：擴張、限制或爲其他變更

constituted：成立

simultaneously：同時

its transmitting manner：傳達方法

concordant intent：一致之意思

essential elements：必要之點

earnest money：定金

presumed to be：推定爲……

intentional or negligent：故意或過失

not predictable：不可預見

performance：履行

rescind the contract：解除契約

without giving the notice：不通知

restore the injured party to the status quo：回復被害人之原狀

exchange：互易

gift：贈與

lease：租賃

loan：借貸

mandate：委任

manager and commercial agents：經理人與代辦商

brokerage：居間

commission agency：行紀

deposit：寄託

warehousing：倉庫

carriage：運送

partnership：合夥

compromise and settlement：和解

guaranty：保證

第三節 習題

選擇題（四選一）

1. If one party has reasonable reliance to his detriment on the promises of the other party, he may request the court to apply _____ to award him a Reliance damages suffered due to his reasonable reliance on the agreement.

   (1) unjust enrichment

   (2) tort

   (3) an equitable doctrine of Promissory Estoppel

   (4) contract

2. A minor can enter into a contract and cancel it, while the other party (adult) _____.

   (1) is bound by the contract

   (2) can cancel it too

   (3) can ask for damages

   (4) can ask the minor to pay

3. The contract of sale of a piece of land should be _____.

   (1) in writing

   (2) registered

   (3) motorized

   (4) publicized

4. In U.S., building is considered as _____.

   (1) a property

   (2) movable estate

   (3) a part of land

   (4) separate real estate from the land

5. The capacity of a minor, under U.S. law, is _____.

    (1) like an adult

    (2) divided into several stages according to age

    (3) uniform

    (4) one category, not classified according to age into several stages like our Civil Code

6. When the purpose of a contract becomes incapable of completion, it may constitute _____ and make the contract come to an end.

    (1) voidable contract

    (2) void contract

    (3) frustration of purpose

    (4) act of god

7. When the debtor repudiate a contract beforehand, the aggrieved party _____.

    (1) can ask him paying damages

    (2) has duty to mitigate damages

    (3) can do nothing

    (4) wait and see

8. Failure to carry out a promise to make a gift cannot be enforceable as a breach of contract because _____.

    (1) lack of consideration

    (2) not notarized

    (3) not in writing

    (4) many consideration

9. Parole evidence rule means _____.

    (1) subject to change

    (2) all set

    (3) all evidence are admissible

    (4) the written contract is the only basis concerning the rights and duties of both parties, no additional or different evidence can be admitted

10. A third-party beneficiary is found in _____ contract that requires the payment of death benefits to a third party. That third party does not sign the contract and may not even be aware of its existence, yet is entitled to benefit from it.

(1) travel

(2) medical

(3) publishing

(4) life insurance

11. Under U.S. law, acceptance takes effect on _____.

(1) receiving by the offeror

(2) dispatching by the acceptor

(3) nodding

(4) calling

12. A sold a piece of land to B. A refused to deliver it to B. The best remedy for B is suing A based on _____.

(1) injunction

(2) right of specific performance.

(3) punitive damages

(4) penalty clause

13. Quasi-contract means _____.

(1) unjust enrichment

(2) mandate

(3) standardized contract

(4) a tort

14. An "Act of God" mean _____.

(1) natural occurring events

(2) war

(3) disaster

(4) both naturally occurring events and events due to human intervention

15. A tsunami is a _____ .

    (1) force majeure

    (2) act of god

    (3) both act of god & force majeure

    (4) war

16. A owed B $500. Later B agree to accept a book worth $250 in exchange for discharging the debt. Can B sued for the other $250? Ans: _____ .

    (1) Yes

    (2) No. Because accord and satisfaction substituted the original debt

    (3) It is an exchange

    (4) It is a novation

17. A contract contains a unilateral mistake that was _____ and the other party knew or should have known of the mistake. The mistaken party may revoke the contract.

    (1) attached to the agreement

    (2) material to the agreement

    (3) immaterial

    (4) element

18. Due to the possibility of unequal bargaining power, unfairness, and unconscionability, in some cases, courts look at _____ with a special scrutiny.

    (1) certain contracts

    (2) adhesion contracts

    (3) unilateral contracts

    (4) coercion

19. A _____ is an event which must take place before a party to a contract performs or does his part.
    (1) condition impossible
    (2) condition subsequent
    (3) condition concurrent
    (4) condition precedent

20. _____ is an event or state of affairs that, if it occurs, will terminate one party's obligation to the other.
    (1) Condition impossible
    (2) Condition subsequent
    (3) Condition concurrent
    (4) Condition precedent

21. Negotiations are just a lot of _____ exchanged between the parties.
    (1) talks
    (2) offers
    (3) counter-offers
    (4) consideration

▲選擇題解答
1. (3)　2. (1)　3. (1)　4. (3)　5. (4)　6. (3)　7. (2)　8. (1)　9. (4)
10. (4)　11. (2)　12. (2)　13. (1)　14. (1)　15. (3)　16. (2)　17. (2)　18. (2)
19. (4)　20. (2)　21. (3)

第四節　詞彙整理

一、同義詞

adopt－enact－promulgate－legislate－pass－originate－model

revoke－rescind－remission－

prescribed by－governed by－governing law

opinion－honer－acknowledge

form contract－contract of adhesion

receive－consent

assent－consent

detriment－harm－loss

unless－otherwise－provided－except

agency－agent

rescind－rescission

reject－rebut－refuse－deny

ordain－order－adjudicate

imposed－charge

ratify－approve－confirm－acknowledge－ratification

necessary－indispensable

reject－rejection

revoke－rescind－withdraw

follow－compliance－comply－according to－pursuant to－in accordance with

contemplate－anticipate

supersede－substitute－replace

condition subsequent－condition precedent

alteration－modify－change－alter－revise

二、類似詞

duress－undue influence

subject to－vulnerable to

title－ownership－possession

form－formality

ingredients－element

specific－particular

void－voidable

unequal－unfairness－unconscionable

contract－promissory estoppel－mutual assent

expectation－reliance

restatement－code

focus－emphasize

minor－minority

equity－fairness

warranty－condition－warrant

public policy－moral

novation－assignment

accord and satisfaction－performance

deem－presume

delegated－assign－assigned

statute of limitation－prescription

lease agreement－landlord and tenant

reward－prize

mandate－order

substantially－basically－primarily

三、反義詞

infant; adult

offer; accept; acceptance

offer; counteroffer

offerer; offeree

insane; incompetent

offer; counteroffer

offerer; offeree

valid; invalid

enforceable; unenforceable

express; implied; explicit

principal; agent

real estate; personal estate

agree; disagree; dissent

express; implied warranty

revocable; irrevocable

objective; subjective

express; implicit; implied

四、詞性轉換

（一）動詞 → 名詞

promise → promissory, promisee, promisor

interpret → interpretation

accept → acceptance

presume → presumption

terminate → termination

prescribe → prescription

consider → consideration

misrepresent → misrepresentation

coerce → coercion

agree → agreement

perform → performance

deliver → delivery

forbid, prohibit → disallow, proscribe, ban, prohibition, forbiddance

（二）形容詞 → 名詞

private → privacy, privity

charitable → charity

injunctive → injunction

legal → legality

optional → option

capable → capacity

able → ability

mutual → mutuality

equal → equality

conditional → condition

fraudulent → Fraud

第三章 ▌ 侵權行為

第一節 美國法

一、緒言

Tort is one of the basic area of laws in U.S. law. It is also an important source of civil litigation. It is a part of law rather than a part of general part of law of obligation as in civil law countries. Its contents and applications are much wider than our law. Basically tort law belongs to common law, state law. In recent years, certain statutes are passed, and however, they are mostly limited to procedural aspect.

Tort and contract often overlapped. The scope of tort liability are wider than contract. The victims may claim spiritual damages or punitive damages whereas they can not do so in contractual cases. The victims may choose between these two options and often based on tort.

美國之侵權行為法為基本法律領域之一，侵權行為（尤其車禍）也是民事訴訟之主要來源，侵權行為法在法律中自成一領域，與在大陸法只是債編通則之一部不同，其內容遠比我國民法債編侵權行為有關規定複雜，適用範疇亦更廣。且各種侵權行為之要件與效果各異，共同適用之原則似不太多。基本上侵權法為普通法，且為州法，近年雖有通過制定法，但多涉及程序方面。

侵權行為常與契約法重疊，侵權責任範圍較契約責任為廣，可請求賠償精神損害或懲罰性賠償，而契約案件原告原則上不能。被害人常可在契約請求與侵權請求之間選擇請求，此時似常以侵權行為提出請求。

二、特色

1. Misrepresentation may also constitute a tort.
   過失甚至無辜之不實表述（misrepresentation）亦可能負擔侵權行為責任。

2. To induce the debtor to breach a contract by a third party may constitute a tort.
   第三人勸誘債務人不履行債務（毀約）亦可能成立侵權行為。

3. Malicious prosecution may constitute a tort.
   健訴濫訟易構成侵權行為。

4. The U.S. has long recognized invasion of privacy as a tort.
   美國很早就承認侵害隱私權為侵權。

5. The U.S. recognize manufacturers' strict liability system.
   美國法承認產品製作人之無過失賠償責任。

6. The victim of tort has a duty to mitigate the damages.
   侵權行為之被害人有減少（mitigate）損害之義務。

7. The U.S. law permits punitive damages.
   准許懲罰性損害賠償。

8. In malpractice cases, U.S. has changed victim consent to informed consent recently.
   業務過失案件，近來被害人同意免責一點，已改為須知情同意（informed consent）。

9. The U.S. has developed Assumption of the risk theory.
   發展出被害人承擔風險（自甘冒險，Assumption of the risk）之理論。

10. In U.S. the development of workers' compensation decreased the number of tort cases in recent years.
    近年來由於保險制度〔尤其勞工災害保險（workers' compensation）〕發展之影響，減少了侵權行為法之應用。

三、介紹

A tort is an act or omission that gives rise to injury or harm (property, health, or well-being) to another and the injured party can sue for damages in the form of monetary compensation, injunction and restitution.

侵權行為是導致他人損害（財產、健康或福祉）之作為或不作為，被害人可訴請金錢賠償、發禁制令與回復原狀。

（一）Torts' Elements 侵權行為之要素

The elements of torts are: duty, breach of duty, causation and injury. Sometimes a wrongful act may be both a criminal and tort case.

侵權行為之要素有：義務、違反義務、因果關係及損害。有時一個違法行為同時構成犯罪與侵權行為。

（二）Torts' Categories 侵權行為的類型

1. Intentional Torts 故意侵權行為

An individual or entity purposely engages in conduct that causes injury or damage to another, e.g., intentionally hitting a person.

指個人或團體故意從事導致傷害或損害他人之行為，如故意撞人。

2. Negligent Torts 過失侵權行為*

They occur when the defendant's actions were careless, e.g., causing an accident by failing to obey traffic rules.

指被告行為欠缺注意，例如不守交通規則引起事故。

*按過失在我國法與故意並列為主觀責任形態，但在美國法除與故意並列為主觀責任形態外，也作為一種侵權行為之名稱。

3. Strict Liability Torts 無過失侵權行為

Impose liability without regard to the defendant's level of care. No need to prove that he acted negligently. Including:

(1) liability for making and selling defective products (Products Liability): Defects in design, manufacturing defects, and warning defects. Because a business entity is often in a better economic position to bear (or insure against) a loss caused a defective product than consumer.

(2) liability for abnormally dangerous activities: such as fearful animals.

課予責任而不問被告注意程度如何，無需證明行為人過失，包括：

(1) 製售有瑕疵之產品（產品製作人責任）：在設計、生產及警告上有過失。因廠商在經濟上常比消費者較能承受（或投保）瑕疵產品之損失。

(2) 異常危險活動之責任：例如猛獸。

（三）Requirement of Liability 責任之要件

1. Duty to Protect Another 防護他人之義務

If a special relationship exists, the defendant has a duty to aid or protect another.

Besides, if one puts another in peril, assumes a duty through contract, or begins to assist and then backs out, one has duty to aid, if breached, negligence could ensue.

如有特殊關係（如救生員）存在，則被告有協助或保護他人之義務。

又如因自己行為致他人處於危險，或由契約負有義務時，則負救援之義務，否則可能負過失責任。

2. Negligence Per Se 行為本身有過失

It is a theory in personal injury law that a person is presumed to have acted negligently if he injures someone in the course of violating a statute.

如行為人違反法令，傷害他人，則推定其有過失，此為人身傷害法之原則。

3. Possessor of Land's Duty 土地占有人之責任

The amount of duty owed by possessors in terms of importance is first to (1) invitees, then (2) licensees, the lowest is owed to (3) trespassers.

土地占有人對他人進入其土地受到傷害之責任，按重輕依次為：(1)對受邀人；(2)對允許進入之人；(3)對闖入人。

4. Res Ipsa Loquitor (the thing speaks for itself) 讓證據說話之原則

Permits plaintiffs to circumstantially prove negligence if the following are proved: (1)the defendant had exclusive control over (the allegedly defective) product during manufacture, (2) under normal circumstances, the plaintiff would not have been injured by the product if the defendant had exercised ordinary care, and (3) the plaintiff's conduct did not contribute significantly to the accident. While res ipsa loquitor does not necessarily lead to definitive proof of negligence, it does permit jurors to infer a fact for which there is no direct, explicit proof-the defendant's negligent act or omission.

原告如能證明：(1)被告在製造時完全控制該有瑕疵之物；(2)正常情形，被告如實施通常注意，則原告不致因該物受到損害；(3)原告對事故並無重大之與有過失時，則可依情況證據，證明被告有過失。被告雖無直接明確過失作為或不作為之證據，但此理論准許陪審團推論被告有過失。

5. Proximate Cause 相當因果關係

The accident and injury must be shown to be the natural and probable result of the act(s) of negligence committed. Most involve some form of foreseeability.

事故與損害須是過失行爲之自然與可能之結果。行爲人對其行爲之結果多須有預見可能性。

6. A Prima Facie Case 表面證據

In order to prove that the defendant committed a tort, a plaintiff needs to prove that a defendant has met all the components of a prima facie tort case and justify a verdict in his favor, provided such evidence is not rebutted by the other party.

爲了證明被告作了侵權行爲，原告須證明被告已符合表面侵權行爲的要件，如對造未能駁倒此種證據，則可勝訴。

（四）Examples of Intentional Torts 故意侵權行爲之事例

1. Nuisance 干擾

(1) Public Nuisance 公共干擾

A public nuisance is when a person unreasonably interferes with a right that the general public shares in common.

公共干擾乃無理干擾公眾享有之權利。

(2) Private Nuisance 私人干擾

A private nuisance is when the plaintiff's use and enjoyment of his land is interfered with substantially and unreasonably through a thing or activity.

私人干擾係指由於某人之某物或活動，干擾他人對土地之用益至重大且無理之程度。

The court may grant injunctive relief if remedy is not adequate.

如賠償不足彌補損失，則法院可頒發禁制令。

2. Conversion 侵占

Unauthorized act depriving an owner of possession of tangible personal property.

侵占乃無故剝奪所有人對有形動產之占有。

3. Defamation 妨礙名譽

Intentionally make malicious statements, spoken or written, that injure another person's reputation. The truth of the statement is a complete defense.

妨礙名譽乃惡意以言詞或文字陳述妨礙他人之名譽，如證明所指屬實，則可免責。

4. Interference with Contract Relations 干預契約關係

A third person maliciously and substantially interferes with the contract relations (the performance) between contracting parties.

干預契約關係係指第三人惡意且重大干擾當事人之間契約關係之履行。

5. False Imprisonment 妨礙自由

Unlawfully deprive the victim of his freedom of movement

妨礙自由乃違法剝奪被害人之行動自由。

6. Infliction of Emotional Distress 使人身心受創

Engaging in extreme and outrageous conduct intended to cause another person severe mental anguish.

使人身心受創，乃以極端與惡劣之行為，使他人心靈嚴重受創。

7. Invasion of Privacy 妨礙隱私

Unwarranted publicity that places the plaintiff in a false light, intrudes into the plaintiff's private life, discloses embarrassing private facts, or uses the plaintiff's name or likeness for defendant's gain.

妨礙隱私乃無故公開抹黑原告、闖入原告之私生活、揭露使人困窘之私人事實，或用原告之姓名或肖像獲利。

8. Malpractice 業務過失

Professionals fail to use higher degree of knowledge, skills, or experience than a reasonable person.

業務過失乃專業人士怠於實施較合理之人*更高程度之知識、技能或經驗。

*所謂合理之人（a reasonable person），與我國法上之善良管理人相當。

9. Malicious Prosecution 濫控

Maliciously and without probably cause in filing a criminal prosecution

濫控乃惡意無故提起刑事告訴。

（五）Defenses 免責事由（Affirmative Defenses 積極抗辯）

1. Consent 同意

The victim's consent is an affirmative defense that may be available to the wrongdoer sued for an intentional tort. Consent can be given expressly in writing or verbally, and can also be implied by conduct.

同意乃加害人被控故意侵權行為時，可以被害人有同意，作為抗辯。同意除書面或言詞明示外，亦可由行為加以默示。

2. Self-defense 正當防衛

Typically a defense to battery. Similar to self-defense is the defense of others.

正當防衛通常係針對傷害之抗辯，為了防衛他人，亦然。

3. Defense of Property 防衛財產

Typically a defense to trespass to land or trespass to chattels.

防衛財產通常係對他人闖入土地或擅用動產之抗辯。

4. Necessity 緊急避難

(1) Private Necessity 私下緊急避難

E.g., in order to escape a blizzard while hiking break into the barn to stay safe.

例如遠足時,闖入無人之穀倉,躲避冰雹。

(2) Public Necessity 公共緊急避難

E.g., firefighters or police officers damage someone's property to prevent harm to the greater community (fire) or chase a dangerous criminal.

例如消防人員或員警為了防止對社區更大損害(如火災)或追捕危險犯人而損壞他人財產。

5. Duress 脅迫

The defendant committed a crime because someone directly forced them to do it.

被告受他人直接脅迫而犯罪。

6. Assumption of the Risk 承擔風險

The victim had knowledge of the risk and made the free choice of exposing to it.

被害人知悉風險而自甘冒險。

(六) Some Problems Concerning Liability 有關責任之問題

1. Contributory Negligence vs. Comparative Negligence 與有過失 與比較過失

Contributory negligence is a rule that prevents an injured party from collecting any money in a lawsuit if he had the slightest fault in an accident. This is too harsh for the injured party. Many states nowadays follow the rule of comparative negligence, allowing damages to be awarded based on each party's share of the fault. E.g., a plaintiff adjudged 80% responsible for his injuries would still be able to collect 20%.

依與有過失之原則，被害人如對事故有一絲過失，即不能在訴訟獲得賠償，因此對被害人過苛。許多州現今採比較過失原則，可按雙方過失比例使被害人獲得賠償。例如原告被判對其傷害要負80%責任時，仍可獲得20%賠償。

2. Imputed Negligence 轉嫁過失

Employers are liable for his employees' torts committed in the scope of their employment. (The agent acts for the principal.)

因代理人爲本人行動，雇用人須對受雇人職務上所爲之侵權行爲負責。

3. Apply Transferred Intent Doctrine 適用轉移故意理論

Transferred intent is used when a defendant intends to harm one victim, but then unintentionally harms a second victim instead. Namely, intent can be transferred from one victim to another, even if the actual victim is one other than the intended target of the original tort. (The person is legally responsible as long as he or she knew such action would harm someone.)

故意可自一被害人移轉至另一人，即使眞正被害人並非原來侵權行爲之目標。*當被告欲傷害某被害人而無意傷害到別的被害人時，可適用轉移故意理論（只要該人知悉其行爲會傷到人，即須負法律責任）。

*此點與美國刑法規定相同。

（七）Remedies 救濟

1. Compensatory Damages 補償性賠償

Equal to the monetary value of the injured party's loss of earnings, loss of future earning capacity, and reasonable medical expenses. Thus, courts may award damages for incurred as well as expected losses, may also recover noneconomic damages to compensate the plaintiff's pain and suffering.

相當於請求喪失之收入、喪失將來賺錢能力及合理醫療費之金錢。因此法院可命被告賠償原告已蒙受以及期待之損失，有時亦可請求非經濟損失，以補償原告之精神苦痛。

2. Punitive Damages 懲罰性賠償

When the court wants to deter future misconduct, it may award punitive damages in addition to compensatory damages. In a case of a defectively manufactured product, award punitive damages to compel the manufacturer to use more care in production.

當法院欲嚇阻將來不法侵權行為時，除科補償性賠償外，可另科懲罰性賠償。例如對有瑕疵之製品可科以此種賠償，使製造商日後生產時實施較高之注意。

3. Injunction 禁制令

The injured party may apply for an injunction if he can prove that he will suffer irreparable harm without the court's intervention.

被害人如能證明非經法院介入，會受到難以彌補之損害時，可申請發出禁制令。

（八）其他有關問題

1. Breach of Contract 契約不履行

A breach of contract is not considered a tortious act.

契約之不履行並非侵權行為。

2. Tort Reform 侵權制度之改革

Recently calls for reform of tort law are high. In the U.S. reform has focused on lawsuits related to medical claims and healthcare costs (the unnecessary use of costly medical tests and the high price of drugs due to patents).

近年改革侵權法呼聲高漲。在美國，侵權行為法之改革，主要針對醫療請求與醫療支出之訴訟（包括使用不必要的高昂醫事檢查與高價之專利藥品）。

3. Last Clear Chance 最後明顯機會之原則

This rule was created by judges to ease the harsh effects of contributory negligence. If the plaintiff can prove that, as between the plaintiff and the defendant, the defendant was the one who had the last opportunity to change course and avoid injuring the plaintiff.

此原則係由法官所創設，旨在緩和昔日與有過失原則不賠之嚴苛。如原告能證明被告是原被二人之間有最後機會改變行駛路線，以避免傷害原告時，原告仍可獲得賠償。

4. Informed Consent 知情同意

In malpractice cases, for consent to be valid, instead of mere consent, the person must have informed consent. Namely, he should be given all information about the treatment, including its benefits and risks, any alternative, and what will happen if treatment does not go ahead.

在業務過失案件，被告要主張被害人同意之抗辯，如僅病人單純之同意，仍嫌不足，尚需有所謂知情同意，即醫師需對病人告知手術之全部資訊，包含利益與風險、有無其他選擇，以及不手術之後果。

5. Class Action 集體訴訟

America law recognize class action.

承認集體訴訟（詳見民事訴訟法部分）。

（注）本文參考

1. https://www.law.cornell.edu/wex/tort
2. Introduction to Tort Law
   https://fas.org/sgp/crs/misc/IF11291.pdf
3. GENERAL LAW OF TORTS
   https://courses.lumenlearning.com/suny-monroe-law101/
   chapter/general-law-of-torts/

四、詞彙

tort：侵權行為

held legally accountable：法律上負責（被究責）

breach of duty：違反義務

causation：因果關係

a wide range：大範圍

personal injury cases：人身傷害案件

strict liability：絕對（無過失）責任

negligence：過失侵權行為

defective product：有瑕疵產品

negligence per se：法律上當然過失

prime examples：主要例子

establish：證明

the product in question：該產品

wrongful act：不法行為

criminal charges：刑事追訴

assault and battery：傷害（毆打）

false imprisonment：妨礙自由

conversion：侵占

intentional infliction of emotional distress：故意使人精神頹喪

fraud / deceit：詐欺、欺騙

trespass：侵入

trespass (to land and property)：非法侵入（土地或財產）

tortfeasor：侵權人

assumption of risk：自甘冒險

deceit：詐欺

defamation：妨礙名譽

slander：誹謗

trespass to chattel：無故使用他人動產

business torts：商業侵權行為

economic torts：經濟侵權行為

joint tort：共同侵權行為

mitigate：減輕

doctrine of Res Ipsa Loquitur：讓證據說話之原則

last clear chance：最後顯然之原則

malicious prosecution：誣告

personal injury：人身傷害

preponderance of evidence：有優勢的證據

public nuisance：公共干擾

public necessity：公共緊急避難

private necessity：私人緊急避難

mistake：錯誤

misrepresentation：不正表述

gross negligence：重大過失

a reasonable person：合理之人

excuse / immunity：免責

prima facie case：表面案件

duty of care：注意義務

licensee：被授權人

invitee：被邀之人

class action：集體訴訟

malpractice：業務過失

informed consent：有資訊之同意

restitution：回復原狀

interference with economic relation：干預經濟關係

wrongful death：違法致人於死

nuisance：干擾

malicious prosecution：濫告

self help：自助行為

contributory negligence：與有過失

comparative negligence：比較過失

deliberate：蓄意

wanton：放肆

willful：有意

reckless：毫不在意

punitive damages：懲罰性賠償

第二節　我國法

一、特色

1. The victims of torts have no duty to mitigate their damages.
   侵權行為之被害人無減少（mitigate）損害之義務。

2. The tort liability of the possessor of a real estate does not have so many classifications as American law.

不動產占有人或所有人侵權行爲並不如美國法細分保管責任。

3. Those who are guilty of contributory negligence may get redress depending upon each case.

與有過失被害人不致全無救濟。

4. Our Civil Code does not have punitive damages.

民法尚未建立懲罰性損害賠償制度。

5. It is rare to claim tort liability by asserting malicious prosecution.

健訴濫訟似不易構成侵權行爲。

6. In malpractice cases, the law has not changed victim's consent to informed consent.

業務過失案件，被害人同意免責，尚未改爲知情同意（informed consent）。

二、詞彙

instigators and accomplices are deemed to be joint tortfeasors：教唆與幫助視爲共同侵權人

privacy or chastity：隱私或貞操

taking of proper measures：採取適當措施

intentionally or negligently：故意或過失

rehabilitation of his reputation：回復名譽

enacted：制定

is bound to compensate：應賠償

jointly liable：連帶負責

tortfeasors：侵權人

instigators and accomplices are deemed to be joint tortfeasors：造意人與幫助人視爲連帶侵權人

breach of duty：違反義務

arising therefrom / arising from it：由此所生

obviate the injury：減輕損失

wrongfully damaged：不法侵害

capable of discernment：能識別

at the time of committing the act：行為時

exercise of reasonable supervision：實施合理監督

injured person：被害人、受損人

wrongfully caused：違法引起

occasioned：發生

provision of the preceding sentence：前條規定

specified in：訂在

in the performance of his duties：執行職務中

on the application of：基於……之請求

claim for reimbursement：求償

possessor：所有人

occasioned：引起

reasonable care.：相當注意

claim for reimbursement：求償

excitement or provocation：挑動、惹起

defective construction or insufficient maintenance：瑕疵設置或保管不足

defectiveness in the production, manufacture, process, or design of the merchandise：產品在生產、製造、加工或設計上有瑕疵

inconsistent with：不一致

unless otherwise provided by the act：除法律另有規定外

according to the ordinary course of things：依通常情形

incurring the medical expenses：支出醫藥費

increasing the need in living：增加生活上之需要

incurring the funeral expenses：支出殯葬費

deceased：死者

statutorily bound to furnish maintenance：法律上須扶養……

purely pecuniary loss：純粹金錢損失

第三節　習題

選擇題（四選一）

1. A was injured by using certain goods manufactured by B's company. A claimed B's merchandise was defective in manufacturing based on product liability. A has _____ B's fault.

   (1) to prove

   (2) no need to prove

   (3) option to prove

   (4) no remedy at all

2. A sued B for defamation. B claimed he was not liable because _____.

   (1) a was at fault

   (2) he can prove the fact he stated was true

   (3) he heard from a third party

   (4) he has no intention to offend A

3. A, a medical doctor, was sued for malpractice by his patient B. If A wants to be free of liability he should prove _____.

   (1) he had used a reasonable man's care

   (2) he had used his higher (professional) degree of care

   (3) he is not intentional

   (4) he is not negligent

4. A was annoyed by the smell and noise coming from his neighbor B's land. A has the remedy against B based on _____.

   (1) strict liability

   (2) nuisance

   (3) privacy

   (4) fame

5. A was followed by B for several days. A can seek remedy based on

_____.

(1) invasion of freedom

(2) invasion of privacy

(3) assault

(4) invasion of free will

6. A went to a circus and touched a tiger. He was bitten by the tiger. He might not get damages because his action was _____.

(1) negligent

(2) too risky

(3) intentional

(4) assumption of the risk

7. In B, a fast food store, the floor was too slippery, and a customer A slip and fall. A can sue for B's _____.

(1) intentional

(2) negligence

(3) strict liability

(4) accident

8. When the court wants to deter future misconduct, it may award __

____ in addition to compensatory damages.

(1) warning

(2) fine

(3) punitive damages

(4) community service

9. In _____ cases the victim does not need to prove that the manufacturer's negligence.

(1) dangerous

(2) strict liability

(3) negligence

(4) willful

10. A was invited by B for a party. A was injured due to a hole in the garden which B did not call A's attention of it. B was liable based on _____.
    (1) negligence
    (2) A was an invitee
    (3) A was a trespasser
    (4) assumption of risks

11. A drove a car and collided with B's car. Both were a kind of negligence. Can A claim damages from B? on what ground?
    (1) No, comparative negligence.
    (2) Yes, contributory negligence.
    (3) No, assumption of risk.
    (4) Depends on which negligence the state adopts.

12. A fired a gun at B. It missed B but killed a bystander C. A is liable for killing C based on _____.
    (1) assumption of risk
    (2) transferred intent
    (3) men's rea
    (4) negligence

13. The owner of a land is generally not liable for injury sustained by _____.
    (1) a guest
    (2) an invitee
    (3) a trespasser
    (4) a licensee

14. In _____, the victim does not have to prove the negligence of the defendant, because a business entity is often in a better economic position to bear (or insure against) a loss caused by a defective product than consumer.

    (1) minor cases

    (2) tort cases

    (3) Products Liability cases

    (4) civil cases

15. Proximate cause denotes one that the law considers as the primary cause of the plaintiff's injury. Namely, the plaintiff must show that his injuries were _____ without which the injuries would not have happened.

    (1) approximate consequence

    (2) effect

    (3) consequence

    (4) the natural and direct consequence of the proximate cause,

16. In class action,if your class action lawsuit is not successful, you do not have the right _____ at a later date.

    (1) to bring another lawsuit

    (2) to bring an individual lawsuit

    (3) to settle lawsuit

    (4) to terminate lawsuit

17. The injured parties may apply for _____ rather than monetary relief. But he must prove that it would suffer irreparable harm without the court's intervention.

    (1) an injunction

    (2) declaratory judgment

    (3) jury trial

    (4) affidavit

18. If defendant's extreme misconduct causing plaintiff mental suffering (mental worry, distress, grief, and mortification), the plaintiff can recover based on _____ .
    (1) assault
    (2) privacy
    (3) vandalism
    (4) infliction of emotional distress

19. If a construction worker mishandles a crane and destroys a nearby building, the company overseeing the construction will likely face

    _____.
    (1) strict liability
    (2) joint liability
    (3) no liability
    (4) vicarious liability

20. A is B company's driver. One day he hit C when he was on company business. B company is _____ for A's tort.
    (1) not liable
    (2) not guilty
    (3) B was innocent
    (4) liable for A's negligence

▲選擇題解答

1. (2)　2. (2)　3. (2)　4. (2)　5. (2)　6. (4)　7. (2)　8. (3)　9. (2)

10. (2)　11. (4)　12. (2)　13. (3)　14. (3)　15. (4)　16. (2)　17. (1)　18. (4)

19. (4)　20. (4)

第四節 詞彙整理

一、同義詞

pecuniary－monetary

action－suit－lawsuit

violation－invasion－invade

court－forum－venue

endow－entitle－confer

assist－aid

risk－jeopardy

force－strength

fraud－deceit

suffer－sustain

effect－affect－influence

Punitive or exemplary damages

strict－absolute

relief－redress－remedy

damage－injury－loss－harm

fail－failure

willful－reckless－malicious－
    careless－deliberate

false arrest－false imprisonment

harm－loss－infliction

intentional－malicious－pre-
    anticipated－on purpose－
    purposely

defamation－slander－libel

deceit－fraud－cheat

mitigate－abate－ease

absolve－relieve

unlawful－illegal

interfere－obstruct－breach－violate

aggrieved party－victim－injured
    party

impose－charge

gives rise to－cause－resulting－
    ensue－occasion

commit－perpetrate－engage－
    inflict

omission－forbearance

wrongful－unlawful－unreasonable

hit－strike

ordinary－normal irreparable

二、類似詞

misuse－mistake－
    misrepresentation－misconduct

nuisance－trespass－intervention－

interfere－intrude－invasion

self help－self defense－necessity－
    immunity

excuse－justification－defense－
  justify

deliberate－wanton－willful－
  reckless－purposely

privity－contractual

writ－affidavit－summon

suffer－incur

doctrine－theory

issue－controversy－dispute

abnormal－inappropriate

substantially－primarily

exercise－contribute－perform－
  operate－behave

accountable－liable－responsible

三、反義詞

plaintiff; defendant

intentional; accidental

proper; improper

contributory negligence; comparative
  negligence

unauthorized; authorize

四、詞性轉換

（一）動詞 → 名詞

serve → service

injure → injury

omit → omission

require → requirement

provoke → provocation

compensate → compensation

contribute → contribution

harass → harassment

relate → relation → relationship

refer → reference

issue → issuance

proceed → process → procedure →
  proceeding

recover → recovery

presume → presumption

revoke → revocation

transmit → transmission

supervise → supervision

assume → assumption

（二）名詞 → 形容詞

account → accountable (n. accountability)

cause → causal

liability → liable

majority → major

minority → minor

negligence → negligent

intention → intentional

accident → accidental

tort → tortious

money → monetary

act → actual

malice → malicious

negligence → negligent

profession → professional

essence → essential

substance → substantial

tort → tortious

compensate → compensatory

Proximation → proximate

contribution → contributory

（三）形容詞 → 名詞

private → privacy

public → publicity

risky → risk

abusive → abuse

defensive → defense

intentional → intent

第四章　物權法

第一節　美國法

一、特色

1. Land ownership in American law is extremely complex, based on feudal categories inherited from English law. The law in most states have not been simplified to reflect modern circumstances.

　美國不動產法受英國封建制度與封建土地制度影響太深，未能簡化反映現代社會，極為複雜。*

　　* 英美土地所有權不採物權法定主義，土地所有權不但在時間上，而且在質量上都有長短大小不同層次，不需有永久性，可有永遠、終身及定期等種種不同形態。不動產所有權可能包含現存利益、將來利益、占有權等，極其複雜，與大陸法系單純之物權法不可同日而語，對非專門研究英美不動產法之人，極難理解。

2. Unlike our civil code, buildings and other fixtures are considered as a part of the land.

　房屋等土地上之定著物被認為土地之一部，而非獨立之不動產，與我國法不同。

3. Different from our land law, mineral belongs to the owner of the land.

　地下之礦產亦歸土地所有人所有，不似我國歸國民全體所有。

4. Under U.S. law, lease due to the fact that the lessee having possession, is considered as a type of property right, rather than a contract as our law.

租賃由於承租人有占有權，亦被認為一種物權，而非我民法等
大陸法之債權。

5. The conveyance of real estate does not adopt registration system.
The process of investigating clear title is extremely complicated and
time-consuming, causing the development of title insurance.
不動產產權移轉不似我國採登記生效要件，調查產權有無瑕疵
極其繁複，以致產生產權保險（title insurance）之需要，產權保
險公司之發達與廣泛利用成為美國物權法之一大特色。

6. A developer usually imposes a number of restrictive restrictions
(E.g., not to adapt the property for business use, not to structurally
alter the property without the developer's consent.) when selling
off various plots on an estate in order to protect and maintain
the characteristic of the estate as a whole. (These covenants are
enforceable, if they are reasonably necessary to protect legitimate
business interests; and their duration no longer than is necessary to
protect those interests.)
美國地產之開發商出售地產時，為了維護整體地產之特色，常
訂有特殊之限制約款（restrictive covenants），（例如非經其同
意，不可改為商業用途，不可改變結構現狀）。此約款如合理
保護合法商業利益，且期限非過長，可拘束當事人，也拘束後
來之土地所有人，與我國法不同。

7. Different from land law, mortgage and conditional sale are
convenient and dynamic systems of American personal estate law.
與土地法不同，美國動產法有許多靈活簡便之制度，例如動產
抵押權（chattel mortgage）與附條件買賣（conditional sale）。

8. Trust is a part of property law in U.S. as well as a special product of
Anglo-Amercian legal system. There are both legal ownership and
equitable ownership coexistent in one subject matter.
信託為英美物權法之一部，亦為英美法系特殊之產物，標的物

上之所有權分爲法律上所有權與衡平法上所有權。

9. Property law in the states generally originate from the common law and modified by statutes. Since real estate stays in one location, most real estate law is primarily state law, with some federal laws and local laws (such as zoning).

各州財產法通常源於普通法，並由制定法加以修改。由於不動產位置固定，故大多數財產法基本上爲州法，也涉及聯邦法及若干地方法（諸如分區使用）。

10. Ownership of real estate also can be limited by time, as with a life estate that ends upon the death of a specific person. Ownership can be shared in a variety of ways among individuals.

不動產所有權可在時間上加以限制，例如終身財產於特定人死亡時終了。所有權可由許多個人以不同方法分享。

11. Air right and transfer of development rights are recognized in some states in U.S.

空中權與發展權移轉*爲美國一些州所承認。

 * 所謂空中權係指利用全部或部分不動產上空的權力，或在他人土地上空擁有或建造設施之權利。關於空中權及美國物權法之詳情，可參照楊崇森，遨遊美國法，第一冊第七章，美國物權法之原理與運用，頁263以下。

二、詞彙

tenant：承租人

tenancy：租賃關係

lease：租賃

fee simple：英美法上通常最完整之不動產所有權

ownership：所有權

life estate：終身財產

future interest：將來利益

estate for years：定有確定期間之較長期租賃

periodic tenancy：期滿自動更新，直到出租人或承租人通知要終止時消滅之租賃

tenancy at will：不定期限租賃

beneficiary：受益人

legal title：普通法上所有權

equitable title：衡平法上所有權

conveyance：移轉

single ownership：單獨所有權

community property：夫妻共有財產

quiet enjoyment：和平用益

possession：占有

water right：水權

air right：空中權

transfer of development rights：移轉空中發展權

ejectment：收回不動產

unlawful detainer：無權占有

private nuisance：指被惡臭噪音之類無體之物干擾

right to a view：觀景權

easement：地役權

lien：留置權

abate：減少

injunction：禁制令

nuisance：干擾

zoning：分區使用

eminent domain and condemnation：公用徵收

deed：地契

convenant：約款

convenant of warranty：瑕疵擔保約款

fraudulent conveyance：詐害移轉、詐欺脫產

encumbrance：地產上之負擔（如抵押權之類）

escrow：交第三人保管

escrow agent：保管人

title insurance：產權保險

bailmeant：寄託

certificate of title：產權權狀

fixture：定著物

judicial sale / sheriff's sale：司法拍賣

prescription：時效

premises：地產

adverse possession：反對占有（類似我國因取得時效而取得所有權）

common elements：公共設施

warranty of habitability：適於居住之擔保責任

mortgage：抵押權

bailment：寄託

estate planning：資產計畫

zoning：分區使用

feudal categories：封建種類

feudalism：封建社會

the numerus clausus principle：物權法定主義

personal property：動產

intangible property：不動產

structures：定著

bundle of rights：一束權利

easement：地役權

subsurface rights：地下權

mine minerals：開採礦產

life estate：終身財產

deed：契據
Inheritance Laws：繼承法
Environmental Laws：環保法

第二節　我國法

一、特色

1. Our Civil Code adopts the strict numerus clausus principle.
   民法採物權法定主義。

2. Legal ownership of real property is determined by title deeds. The owner must record his ownership rights with the land office.
   不動產所有權取決於所有權狀，所有人須向地政機構登記所有權。

3. Civil Code acknowledges three types of securities rights: pledge, retention and mortgage, pand three kinds of usufruct or use rights: superficies, easement and agricultural right. A hybrid form, dian right, was rarely used.
   民法上有三種擔保物權：質權、留置權、抵押權，以及三種用益物權：地上權、地役權、農育權。界於二者之間的典權很少用到。

4. Land and fixtures are separate real estates, which make superficies, or above ground rights, a crucial right in land use planning.
   土地與定著物是不同的不動產，致地上權成為土地利用計畫上之要角。

5. A fixture owner will need a supercifies to legally use the land underneath his building. Supercifies is legally effective upon registration.
   定著物之所有人需要地上權，以便法律上利用建物下面之土地。

6. Emphyteusis, or permanent tenancy rights, was abolished and replaced by the new agricultural right.

永佃權已經廢止，由農育權取代。

7. Mortgage is very popular property right. We have maximum amount mortgage.

抵押權是受歡迎的物權，我們有最高限額抵押。

8. Lease is a type of contract under Civil Code. When using temporary immovable property, many people use leases, which have only in personam effect.

租賃在民法是一種契約，當利用一時不動產時，許多人利用租賃，它只是一種債權。

二、詞彙

title deeds (document of deed)：所有權狀

usufruct：用益物權

superficies / above ground rights：地上權

easement：地役權

agricultural right：農育權

emphyteusis or permanent tenancy rights：永佃權

fixture：地上物、定著物

leases：租賃權

in personam effect：債權效力

superficies and its in rem effect：地上權及其物權效力

implemented：施行

easements (or servitudes)：地役權

securities rights：擔保權

pledge：質權

retention：留置權

hypothec：抵押權

maximum amount mortgage：最高限額抵押

strict numerus clausus principle：物權限定主義

ease the accessory principle：放寬從屬性原則

the loan contract：貸款契約

dian right：典權

第三節 習題

選擇題（四選一）

1. _____ is a part of property law in U.S. Here both legal ownership and equitable ownership exist in one subject matter.

   (1) Lease

   (2) Lien

   (3) Trust

   (4) Mortgage

2. Unlike our civil code, _____ belongs to the owner of the land, rather than the people as a whole.

   (1) fixtures

   (2) mineral

   (3) building

   (4) fruits

3. _____ in American law is extremely complex, based on feudal categories inherited from ancient English law.

   (1) Patent

   (2) Intellectual law

   (3) Land ownership

   (4) Environment law

4. Under American law, fixtures like building is considered as _____
   land.
   (1) a part of
   (2) separate and distinct from
   (3) price of
   (4) mixed with

5. Different from land law, _____ mortgage and conditional sale are
   convenient and dynamic systems of American personal estate law.
   (1) foreclosure of
   (2) maximum amount
   (3) first
   (4) chattel

6. _____ right and transfer of development rights are recognized in
   some states in U.S.
   (1) Mineral
   (2) Air
   (3) Lease
   (4) Easement

7. Under U.S. law, lease due to the fact that the lessee having
   possession, is considered as a type of property right, rather than a __
   ____ as our law.
   (1) use and quiet enjoyment
   (2) possession
   (3) ownership
   (4) contract

8. Under our property law of civil code, as far as the type of real property is concerned, we adopt the _____ principle.

   (1) good faith

   (2) numerus clausus

   (3) possession

   (4) collateral

9. _____ is the power of the government to take private property and convert it into public use. The government may only exercise this power if they provide just compensation to the property owners.

   (1) Condemnation

   (2) Eminent Domain

   (3) Compensation

   (4) Deprivation

10. Sale of land or building are often subject to a number of _____, which limit not only the other party but also limit future land owners what he is able to do with the property.

   (1) prescription

   (2) special condition

   (3) restrictive covenants

   (4) terms

▲選擇題解答

　1. (3)　　2. (2)　　3. (3)　　4. (1)　　5. (4)　　6. (2)　　7. (4)　　8. (2)　　9. (2)

　10. (3)

第四節　詞彙整理

一、同義詞

covenant－agreement

二、詞性轉換

（一）動詞 → 名詞

eject → ejectment, ejection

abate → abatement

encumber → encumbrance

advise → advice

detain → detainer

prescribe → prescription

possess → possession

enjoy → enjoyment

survive → survivorship

part → partition

convey → conveyance

condemn → condemnation

reverse → reversal

restrict → restriction

（二）名詞 → 形容詞

part → partial

equity → equitable

adversary → adverse

equity → equitable

fraud → fraudulent

eminence → eminent

habitability → habitable

owner → ownership → own

period → periodic

（三）動詞 → 形容詞

restrict → restrictive

（四）動詞或名詞 → 身分類名詞

trespass → trespasser

invite → invitee

license → licensee, licensor

settle → settler

trust → trustee

benefit → beneficiary

mortgage → mortgager, mortgagee

lease → lessor, leasee

第五章　親屬繼承法

第一節　美國法

一、介紹

1. Marriage 結婚

A couple of more than 18 years old, get a marriage license from a state-authorized official and have a wedding ceremony, civil or religious.

結婚須由年滿18歲男女，自州主管官員取得結婚證書並舉行民事或宗教結婚儀式後，始屬完成。

2. Common Law Marriage 普通法結婚

Two people have not purchased a marriage license or had their marriage solemnized by a ceremony is allowed in a minority of states. The couple have to hold themselves out to the public as being married.

有少數州承認普通法婚姻（即二人雖未取得結婚證書與舉行結婚儀式，但對外公開表示已婚）。

3. Prenuptial Agreements 婚前協議

Prenuptial agreements are recognized in all states allowing parties to agree to spousal support and alimony terms in a premarital or postnuptial agreement, if their agreement is prepared in accordance with state and federal law requirements.

婚前協議爲各州所承認，准許當事人訂入扶養配偶及贍養費條款，只要符合州與聯邦法律規定。

4. Marital Property 婚姻財產

Marital property includes all property acquired by either or both spouses during the marriage but excludes "separate property".

婚姻財產包括一方或雙方在婚姻中取得之一切財產，但特有財產除外。

5. Equitable Distribution of Marital Property 適用衡平分配原則

Absent a writing pre-nuptial or post-nuptial agreement, many states apply equitable distribution principles of marital property on the dissolution of a marriage.

除書面婚前協議另有訂定外，許多州在婚姻解消時，婚姻財產之處理適用衡平分配原則。

6. Grounds of Nullity and Annulment of Marriage 婚姻之無效與撤銷原因

(1) incest.

(2) a former marriage is still in force.

(3) a party is under the age of legal consent.

(4) a party was mentally retarded or mentally ill at the time of the marriage.

(5) consent to the marriage was obtained by force, duress, or fraud.

(6) a party was incurably mentally ill for five years.

(1) 亂倫。

(2) 前婚仍有效。

(3) 一方未達法定同意年齡。

(4) 結婚時身心障礙或精神病。

(5) 因暴力、脅迫、詐欺取得結婚同意。

(6) 一方患不治精神病已五年。

7. Support a Child 親子扶養義務

Parents are responsible for providing support to a child under 18 years of age. Absent agreement, a parent cannot be compelled to support a child past the age of 18.

父母扶養子女至18歲，如無約定，不能迫父母扶養18歲以上子女。惟各州法律很難見到扶養父母之規定。

8. Separation 別居

Separation is often the first step toward a divorce. Many states allow formal judicial separation.

別居常是離婚第一步。許多州准許正式司法別居。

9. Domestic Violence 家暴

Stop one spouse from bothering, issue one of three orders: eviction order, cease and desist order, protective order. For domestic violence, restraining order or order of protection is used.

停止一方配偶騷擾，法院可發三種命令之一：驅逐令、停止令、保護令。家暴多用禁止令或保護令。

10. Surrogacy 借腹生子

Surrogacy refers the practice by which a woman becomes pregnant and gives birth to a baby in order to give it to someone who cannot have children. Surrogate parenting contracts are in some states void and unenforceable.

借腹生子係指婦女為了將小孩送給不能生育之人而懷孕生子。借腹生子契約有些州不承認。

11. Legal Grounds for Divorce 法定離婚事由

A no-fault divorce is available in some form in all states; many states also have fault-based grounds. Common grounds for no-fault divorce are "irreconcilable differences" or "incompatibility". The grounds for a fault-based divorce include: adultery, physical cruelty, mental cruelty, attempted murder, desertion, habitual drunkenness, use of addictive drugs, insanity, impotency, and infection of one's spouse with venereal disease.

無過失離婚在各州以某種形式承認，許多州也採過失主義。無過失離婚是夫或妻都不能歸責於他方，讓婚姻破碎。共同的理由是不可協調的差異或難於相容。過失離婚的理由有通姦、虐待、精神虐待、謀殺未遂、遺棄、酗酒、毒癮、精神錯亂、不能人道、使他方配偶染上性病。

12. Divorce Mediation 離婚前和解

Divorce mediation and a court-based mediation program is available.

離婚訴訟有離婚和解與法院內和解計畫鼓勵當事人和解。

13. Division of Assets in Divorce 離婚時資產之分配

According to marital settlement agreement (keep "separate" property).

Most states apply "equitable distribution", divides as it thinks fair. 50-50 or something else. They consider: the amount of nomarital property; each spouse's earning power; services as a homemaker; waste and dissipation; fault; duration of the marriage; and age and health of the parties.

通常配偶可依婚姻財產契約分配財產（可保留特有財產）。

如不能協議，大多數州採衡平原則，按法院認為公平的方式分割，可能是五十對五十或其他，考慮各配偶所有非婚姻財產的數量、各人的賺錢能力、浪費、主持家務之服務、過失、結婚多久、雙方的年齡與健康。

14. Legitimation 準正

The natural father of an illegitimate child can assume rights and duties of a farther by legitimation.

非婚生子女之生父可由準正取得父母之權利與義務。

15. Custody of Children in Adivorce 離婚後子女之監護

If the parents cannot agree on custody of child, the courts consider based on "the best interests of the child".

如父母不能協議子女之監護，則法院基於「小孩之最佳利益」決定監護人，會考慮許多因素。

16. Joint Custody 共同監護

It has two parts: joint legal custody and joint physical custody. Joint legal custody refers to both parents sharing the major decisions affecting the child, including school, etc.

Joint physical custody refers to the time spent with each parent. The amount of time is flexible.

共同監護命令分為共同法律監護與共同監護。共同法律監護指父母二人分擔，如學校等影響小孩的主要決定。

共同監護指子女與各父母一起之時間，可彈性訂定。

17. Child Support in Divorce or Child Support Case 在離婚或子女扶養案件，子女扶養費之決定

State law now places the duty of child support on both parents. When parents divorce, many states use an income shares mode, based on the income of both parents. Some states base upon capability of earning rather than actual earnings. The support may be reduced based upon the amount of time the payor spends with the child.

有些州按付費人收入定扶養費，但許多州基於父母二人之收入，甚至賺錢之能力。扶養費可基於付錢人與小孩共處之時間多少而減少。

18. Failure to Pay Child Support 不付扶養費

Failure to pay court-ordered child support, will be subject to automatic withholding of the obligor's income (hold him in contempt), incarceration, criminal penalties, suspension of driver's licenses and professional licenses, seizure of tax refunds, seizure of bank accounts and investment accounts.

父母不付法院所命子女扶養費時，其執行機制包含：自動扣住義務人之收入、蔑視法庭、羈押、刑罰、停止駕照與職業執照、扣押退稅、扣押銀行帳戶與投資帳戶。

19. Grandparents' Visitation Rights 祖父母探視權

Since 1965, all states have legislation enabling grandparents to petition the courts for visitation rights. Some have extended the right to other relatives.

自1965年起，各州立法，准祖父母申請法院探視孫子女。有些州將此權利擴大到其他親屬。

20. Civil Union or Same-sex Marriages 同性婚姻或伴侶

The so-called civil union is a legally recognized union with rights similar to those of marriage, created originally for same-sex couples in jurisdictions legally disallowed to marry. Certain states now recognizes same-sex marriages, but do not necessarily recognized civil unions contracted within the state.

所謂同性伴侶之權利類似結婚，原為不准結婚之州為此類人而設。有些州現已承認同性婚姻，但未必承認同性伴侶契約。

21. Adoption 收養

Adoption is available to individuals and cohabiting couples. In general, any single adult or a married couple jointly can be eligible to adopt a child.

個人與同居人可收養子女。一單身成人或已婚夫婦可共同收養。*

＊收養須經法院核准，且有機構收養，規定相當周密。

22. Testacy is Advisable 遺囑繼承對被繼承人較有利

Leaving a will can give the deceased more room and freedom to dispose his estate. If there is no will, intestacy law applies. One out of every three American has a will. They select an executer of your estate in their will.

遺囑可予死者處分遺產較多之自由與空間。如無遺囑，才適用法定繼承。美國人每三人中有一人有遺囑。他們在遺囑上指派遺囑執行人。

23. Statutory or Forced Share 特留分

Elective share (statutory or forced share) protects the disinherited surviving spouse.

特留分保障被剝奪繼承之生存配偶。

24. Family Allowance etc. 家庭等津貼

Besides homestead* and exempt property allowances, the law entitles the surviving spouse and children to a family allowance.

除了家宅與免責財產津貼外，法律還往往給生存配偶與子女一種家庭津貼。*

＊homestead allowance 係指大多數州通過法律允許宅地所有人或家長標明一處房屋及土地作為其宅地，在執行其一般債務時，該宅地免予被強制執行。

25. Probate 遺囑驗證

Probate is the legal process of proving a last will, which means verifying that the will is legal and the deceased person's intentions are carried out. Probate also occurs when there is no will and a probate court must decide how to distribute the assets of the deceased's estate.

　　遺囑驗證是檢驗遺囑是否合法及死者遺意是否執行，且當無遺囑而遺囑驗證法院須分配遺產予死者親人時之法律程序。惟頗費時與花錢。

26. Trust 信託

Trust is often used by people to make their estate planning and often used to avoid probate.

　　信託常用以從事資產計畫與避免遺囑驗證。

27. Executer & Administrator 遺囑人與遺產管理人

While executer is responsible to handle the will of the deceased, administrator is supposed to handle the estate of the deceased.

　　遺囑執行人負責執行死者之遺囑，而遺產管理人負責處理死者之遺產。實則二者工作內容相似。^{（注）}

（注）本文參考：

1. FAQs about Family Law
   https://www.americanbar.org/groups/family_law/resources/faqs/

2. Family law in the United States: New York: overview
   by John M Teitler, Nicholas W Lobenthal and Paul D Getzels, Teitler & Teitler, LLP
   https://uk.practicallaw.thomsonreuters.com/1-571-0269?transitionType=Default&contextData=(sc.Default)&firstPage=true

3. Family Law Achievements and Challenges in the United States United Nations Expert Group Meeting May 14-15, 2015 Clare Huntington
   https://www.un.org/esa/socdev/family/docs/egm15/Huntington paper.pdf

二、特色

1. Marriage certificates should be first obtained from state government. Divorce must also be permitted by the court. They are not as free as our law.

   結婚須取得許可證，離婚須經法院准許，不似我國近於放任。但另有所謂普通法結婚，等於承認事實婚。

2. Parents have limited right to discipline their children. The parents are subjected to penalty easily. The government can remove children from unfit parents and place them in foster care.

   父母對子女懲戒權有限，稍有不慎，小孩有被強制帶走安置，甚至受刑罰之虞。政府對不適任之父母，可安排小孩監護或收養，並對特別需要之兒童加以照顧。

3. Children owe no legal obligations toward their parents in poverty. The concept of filial duty is much weaker than our law or even German civil law.

   子女對貧困父母法律上幾無明確扶養義務，倫理思想比我國甚至德國民法淡薄。

4. Adoption must be approved by the court. There are also adoption agencies. There are more protection for the adoptees. Adoption are more common in the U.S. than in Taiwan.

   收養須經法院核准，且有機構收養，公權力介入多，對被收養人較有保障。

5. The best interest of the child is prioritized in family cases. Social welfare officials and social workers play bigger roles in family matters than they do in Taiwan.

   處處以兒童之最佳利益為基調，社會福利與社工人員之權力龐大。

6. In the U.S., the government are very concerned about family matters, such as divorces, adoptions, child welfare, etc. There

are family courts and probate courts handling family matters and inherence cases.

美國重視離婚、收養、扶養子女等家事問題，設有家事法院、遺產檢證法院等處理家事案件。

7. Wills are popular in U.S. as wills are subjected to probate procedures and incur cost and time, many wealthy families tend to resort to trusts to pass their estates to their descendants.

美國人繼承遺產多流行遺囑繼承，遺囑須經法院驗證（耗費時間與費用），許多人用信託逃避遺囑驗證手續。

8. Parents may deprive their children from inheriting their estates without cause.

對子女可不附理由排除其繼承權。

三、詞彙

next of kin：最近親屬

relative：親屬

blood relative：血親

lineal relative：直系親屬

collateral relative：旁系親屬

engagement：訂婚

spouse：配偶

cohabitation：同居

common law marriage：欠缺正式儀式之婚姻

civil partnership：家內合夥

same-sex marriage：同性婚姻

paterity：定父性

illegitimate children：非婚生子女

descendant：子孫

marital property：夫妻財產

marital settlement agreement：婚姻財產契約

property regimes：婚前與婚後夫妻財產契約

nonmarital / separate property：特有財產

community property：共同財產

no-fault divorce：無過失離婚

irreconcilable differences：難以妥協之差異

incompatibility：不協調

adultery：通姦

physical cruelty：虐待

mental cruelty：精神虐待

desertion：遺棄

attempted murder：殺人未遂

habitual drunkenness：習慣性酗酒

use of addictive drugs：毒癮

insanity：精神錯亂

impotent：不能人道

infection：犯了

venereal disease：性病

equitable distribution：衡平分配

earning power：賺錢能力

waste and dissipation：浪費

custody：監護

separation：分居、別居

the best interests of the child：子女之最佳利益

joint custody：共同監護

enforcement mechanisms：執行機制

incarceration：羈押

collaboration：合作

suspension：中止、停止

visitation rights：探視權

support：扶養

nonsupport：不扶養

judicial separation：司法別居

marriage dissolution：婚姻解消

Protection Orders Against Domestic Violence：家暴保護令

termination of parental rights：終止親權

juvenile matters：少年事務

emancipation：解放

approval of underage marriages：批准未達年齡結婚

domicile：住所

visitation rights：探視權

nullity：無效

surrogacy agreement：借腹生子契約

pre- and postnuptial agreements and matrimonial：婚前／後協議

alimony：贍養費

life insurance：人壽保險

custodian：保管人

probate：遺囑驗證

executor：遺囑執行人

administrator：遺產管理人

testator：遺囑人

testament will：遺囑

holographic will：手書遺囑

heir：繼承人

intestacy：無遺囑繼承

descent and distribution：繼承與分配

deceased：死者

inheritance：繼承

estate：遺產

legal representative：法定代理人

no-fault divorce：無過失離婚

guardianship / custody：監護

birth certificate：出生證明

adoption：收養

parental responsibility：父母責任

international abduction：國際誘拐

revocable living trust：可撤銷生前信託

decedent / the deceased：死者

testamentary capacity：遺囑能力

bequest / legacy：遺贈

legatee：受遺贈人

devisee：不動產受遺贈人

disinheritance：剝奪繼承權

revocable：可撤回的

administration：遺產管理

distribution：分配

dower：寡婦分

right of curtesy：鰥夫分

inherence of property：財產繼承

doctrine of escheat：歸國庫

inherence tax / estate tax：遺產稅

probate court：遺囑驗證法院

第二節　我國法

特色

1. Filial duty plays a big part in our family law.
   倫理尤其孝道思想濃厚。

2. The restriction of marriage among relatives is more broad. We also have provisions of engagement (promise to marry).
   禁婚親範圍廣，並有婚約規定。

3. The requirement for marriages and divorces is relatively simple. The law are not protective enough for the weaker party.
   結婚及兩願離婚要件過於簡易放任，致夫妻一時衝動，便要兩願離婚，未遑考慮財產分配與小孩監護，事後可能悔之不及，法律似未盡保護之責。

4. Children are obligated to support their parents when they get old. The scope of people who have support right and owe duty to support are much broader than American law.
   子女須對父母負扶養義務，與美國大異。扶養義務人與權利人範圍廣泛，非美國法所能比擬。

5. Adoptions are subject to increasing legal supervision nowadays.
   收養近年法律漸加強監督。

6. Both Family and Family Meeting (Council) are specially stipulated in our law. This is far different from US law.
   家及親屬會議兩章為我國法特色，與美國法相去極遠。

7. Wills are not popular in our country. And legal succession provisions remain to be developed.
   立遺囑之事例少，但法定繼承規定未必盡屬實際合理，有待研酌。

8. There is no probate system. It is not sufficient enough to protect weaker heirs.

遺產分配與遺囑眞僞，缺乏美國遺囑檢證（probate）制度與遺囑檢證（probate）法院，公權力原則不介入，與美國相反，不足以保護弱小之繼承人。

9. Despite so-called equality for both men and women, in reality it is not quite so. In reality male heirs still have advantages due to traditional Chinese culture.

雖說男女平等，但繼承實務上恐難貫徹。

10. The protection for the surviving spouse is not sufficient enough as we do not have homestead allowance.

並無上述美國homestead allowance*之類制度，保護生存配偶不足。

＊ 詳見第105頁第24點。

11. The law lacks preventive measures to prevent heirs from fighting one another.

對防止繼承人爭產，立法缺少預防措施。

12. Trusts and estate planning are still to be fully advocated.

信託與資（遺）產規劃尚待大力提倡。

第三節　習題

選擇題（四選一）

1. ＿＿＿＿＿ is the basic criteria for deciding who gets custody for children in divorce cases.

(1) Stability

(2) The best interests of the child

(3) Love

(4) Security

2. Marriage certificate is a necessary condition for entering into marriage. It can make the couple to consider marriage more _____.

(1) intentionally

(2) quickly

(3) seriously

(4) costly

3. A _____ suit is a legal dispute in which an unwed mother accuses a man of being the father of her child.

(1) parenthood

(2) derivative

(3) paternity

(4) maternity

4. The man whom the deceased appointed in his will responsible to handle and carry out the estate is called _____.

(1) trustee

(2) executer

(3) administrator

(4) conservator

5. The court which handle cases concerning estate and will is called _____.

(1) family court

(2) domestic court

(3) probate court or surrogate's court

(4) district court

6. The man who claim to be the father of an illegitimate child can perform a process called _____ to assume rights and duties of a farther.

   (1) adoption

   (2) maternity

   (3) paternity

   (4) legitimation

7. Leaving a _____ can give the deceased more room and freedom to dispose his estate.

   (1) mandate

   (2) disinheritance

   (3) will

   (4) power of attorney

8. _____ means that the practice by which a woman becomes pregnant and gives birth to a baby in order to give it to someone who cannot have children.

   (1) Stepmother

   (2) Surrogacy

   (3) Donor

   (4) Charity

9. The so-called _____ is a legally recognized union with rights similar to those of marriage, created originally for same-sex couples in jurisdictions where they were not legally allowed to marry.

   (1) partnership

   (2) civil service

   (3) civil union

   (4) close partnership

▲選擇題解答
1. (2)　2. (3)　3. (3)　4. (3)　5. (3)　6. (4)　7. (3)　8. (2)　9. (3)

第四節　詞彙整理

詞性轉換

（一）動詞 → 名詞

adopt → adoption

allow → allowance

execute → execution

administrate → administration

probate → probation

separate → separation

desert → desertion

impotent → impotency

infect → infection

annul → annulment

suspense → suspension

（二）形容詞 → 名詞

null → nullity

incompatible → incompatibility

irreconcilable → irreconcilability

第六章　刑法

第一節　美國法

一、特色

1. The penal law in the U.S. is very strict. Their penalty is harsher than that of most Western countries.

   美國的法律嚴格，刑罰較外國爲重。

2. Crimes are divided into federal crimes and states crimes. Most crimes are governed by state laws, e.g. murder of the President is punished by state law and tried by state court. All federal crimes are statutes. In some states they also punish minor crimes or traffic or building code violations.

   犯罪分爲聯邦犯罪與各州犯罪。大多數犯罪大多適用制定法（刑法典），歸各州管轄（例如謀殺總統係適用州法，歸州法院管轄），聯邦犯罪種類較少，完全是制定法。各州還處罰微罪或違規，例如輕微交通違規或違反建築法規。

3. In certain states vagrancy crime still exist.

   有些州仍有遊蕩罪（vagrancy law）*存在，保障人權不足。

   *所謂遊蕩罪係處罰無固定職業，在公共場所遊蕩之人。

4. U.S. still punishes Conspiracy which is a crime with unclearly defined elements and questionable legal theory and may violate human right.

   美國有犯罪構成要件含糊，且法理有問題之通謀罪（conspiracy），保障人權不足，例如幾年前台灣面板業數家公司被美國司法部以反托拉斯法罪名起訴赴美服刑（詳後）。

5. No reduced penalty for those accused who surrender to the authority voluntarily after committing crimes.
無自首減刑制度。

6. No reduced penalty for the older convicted over eighty of age.
老耄似無減刑規定。

7. Entrapment theory is recognized.
有陷阱理論。

8. Crimes are categorized into felonies and misdemeanors.
犯罪分重罪與輕罪。

9. An abettor is considered an accomplice. This is too lenient and different from us.
教唆犯認為從犯，處罰失之過輕，與我國不同。

10. Whistle-blowers are protected. They have witness and victim protection programs.
鼓勵與保護告密人，有保障證人與犯罪被害人制度。

11. There are contempt of court.
有蔑視法庭罪。

12. Whether those acts following the law, following order of one's superior officer within his job as well as reasonable acts within one's business are exempt from penalty are not clear.
依法令之行為，依所屬上級公務員命令之職務上行為與業務上之正當行為未定為犯罪阻卻之原因。

13. They have obstruction of justice crime.
與我國不同，有妨害司法罪。

14. Murder charges are divided into two different degrees.
謀殺罪分一二兩級。

15. They punish money laundering crimes, computer crimes, organized crimes, terrorism and genocide.
有洗錢罪、電腦及網路犯罪、組織犯罪、反恐怖主義犯罪、種族滅絕罪。

16. Innocent until proven guilty.
有無辜推定。

17. They punished hate crimes.
特別處罰「憎恨罪」＊。

＊由於憎恨或憎惡動機，例如種族、宗教、性向或類似原因，對應
受保護群體之人所加之犯罪，也稱爲「偏見犯罪」。

18. Stalking may constitute a crime.
跟蹤可成立犯罪。

19. There may be no statute of limitation applicable to murder or
kidnapping or murder of first degree.
對謀殺罪之追訴並無時效限制，許多州對擄人勒贖罪亦同。許
多州第一級殺人不能假釋。

20. Those accomplices who served as witness for the country may not
be prosecuted or get pardoned.
對爲國家充當證人之從犯，有不追訴或赦免之作法。

21. Assault and Battery are not very clearly defined. Neither is theft.
傷害（Assault and Battery）之概念不是很明確，又竊盜罪
（theft）之概念與範圍似乎也不是很明確。

22. Death penalty is still recognized by more than thirty states.
仍有三十幾州與聯邦政府有死刑。

23. American law has better protection for child care. Parents may get
into trouble with the law if they commit corporal punishment.
保障兒童福利甚力，父母體罰易吃上官司，此點與我國不同。

24. The judges in deciding sentencing should follow sentencing
guidelines.
爲了避免科刑出入太大，定有量刑指南，限制法官的量刑裁量
權。

25. Most states nowadays adopt indeterminate imprisonment for certain kinds of prisoners.

20世紀後美國大部分州實施不定期刑。但基本上只適用於青少年犯、習慣犯及惡性甚大的犯人，且採用相對不定期刑。

26. The right of carrying guns is guaranteed by the Constitution.

持槍為憲法所保障，不成立犯罪。

27. Cruel and unusual punishment are forbidden.

禁止殘酷與異常之刑罰。

28. The number of Private prisons have been increasing in recent years.

美國私營監獄近年數量增加。

二、介紹

（一）Criminal Law 刑法典

Criminal law is a system of laws concerning punishment of individuals who commit crimes.

刑法乃有關處罰犯罪之人之一套法律。

Each state, and the federal government, decides what sort of conduct to criminalize. Congress makes arson, use of chemical weapons, counterfeit and forgery, embezzlement, espionage, genocide, and kidnapping as federal crimes. Other crimes are left to state. So state penal laws are much more comprehensive than federal law (e.g., murder of the President is a state crime and will be prosecuted by the state).

各州與聯邦政府決定何種行為成立犯罪。美國國會將縱火、使用化學武器、各種偽造、侵占、間諜、種族滅絕及擄人勒贖定為聯邦犯罪。其他犯罪則保留給各州處理，因此各州刑法內容比聯邦法典廣泛的多（例如謀殺總統乃州犯罪，歸各州管轄）。

（二）Elements of a Crime 犯罪之要素

A crime has three elements:

1. Guilty act, namely, the act or omission that was the result of a voluntary bodily movement.
2. The guilty mind or a state of mind to commit a crime. It has three kinds: general intent, specific intent, recklessness/criminal negligence.

犯罪有三要素：

1. 「行爲」指犯罪行爲，即身體自願活動結果之作爲或不作爲。
2. 「犯罪心態」即犯意，分爲：概括犯意、特定犯意及過失三種。

General intent require that the defendant had the intention to commit an illegal act. Specific intent means the defendant objectively desired a specific result to follow his act. Namely, the defendant acted with the intent to achieve a specific goal, in addition to the intent to commit the illegal acts. When a defendant intends to harm one victim, but unintentionally harms a second victim instead. In this case, the defendant's intent transfers from the intended victim to the actual victim and can be used to satisfy the guilty mind element of the crime that the defendant is being charged with. *

Besides, strict liability crimes are crimes for which liability is imposed regardless of his mental state. It's enough for a conviction to prove that the defendant committed it. The example is statutory rape.

概括犯意須被告有意犯某違法行爲。特定犯意指被告客觀上欲其行爲產生特定結果，即除了有意從事某違法行爲外，尚須有意達成特定目的。當被告開槍欲殺甲，卻無意打中乙時，此時被告之故意自甲移轉到乙，而滿足殺傷乙之犯意之要件。*此外制定法犯罪，則不問犯人之心態如何，只須證明有做這行為，即可科以刑責，例如法定強姦。

＊稱為移轉故意之原則（doctrine of transferred intent）

3. Proximate cause means that there is an uninterrupted causal chain between the defendant's act and the harm, and the harm was a foreseeable result of defendant's conduct. One intervening act can break the chain of causation. In criminal case, the government should prove the accused's guilt [beyond a reasonable doubt].

行為與結果之間須有「相當因果關係」，即被告之行為與損害之間須有未中斷之因果關係，且損害乃被告行為之可預見結果。一個介入行為可能使因果關係中斷。在刑事追訴，政府須證明犯人之犯行超過合理懷疑之程度。

（三）Types of Crimes (一) 犯罪之類型（一）

Crimes may be classified into four categories: felonies, misdemeanors, inchoate offenses and statutory crimes.

犯罪可分為四種：重罪、輕罪、不完整犯罪及制定法犯罪。

1. Felonies and Misdemeanors 重罪與輕罪

Misdemeanors are crimes that carry a maximum of one year of jail time and felonies, such as kidnapping, are crimes with punishments in excess of 12 months up to life in prison.

輕罪為監禁一年以下，在普通監牢執行。重罪如擄人勒贖，處徒刑一年以上至無期徒刑，在州監獄執行。

2. Inchoate Crimes 不完整犯罪

Inchoate, or incomplete crimes refers to crimes that were initiated but not brought to completion, including:

不完整犯罪＊指犯罪已發動但未完成，包括：

＊此種分類為我大陸法所不採。

(1) "Attempted" Crimes 未遂犯

Crimes such as attempted robbery, attempted murder, etc..

諸如強盜未遂，謀殺未遂等。

(2) Solicitation 教唆

Crimes involving requesting, asking, hiring, commanding, or encouraging someone else to commit a crime.

觸犯要求、雇用、命令或鼓勵他人犯罪。

(3) Conspiracy 通謀（詳後）

3. Statutory Crimes 制定法犯罪

Statutory crimes are violations of specific state or federal statutes, including property offenses or personal offenses. Eg., alcohol related crimes. Not all crimes are statutory offenses, but many are. Statutory crimes may overlap with other types of crimes.

制定法犯罪係指違反特定之州或聯邦制定法之犯罪，包含財產犯罪或人身犯罪。例如酒精犯罪。並非所有犯罪都是制定法犯罪，但有許多是如此。制定法犯罪可能與別種犯罪重疊。

（四）Types of Crimes (二) 犯罪之類型（二）

Crimes may be categorized into five broad categories.

犯罪又可分爲五大類：

1. Personal Crimes 人身犯罪

Personal crimes are most commonly generalized as a violent crime that causes physical, emotional, or psychological harm to the victim. They include but not limited to:

人身犯罪常指導致被害人身體、情緒或心理損傷之暴力犯罪。包括但不限於：

(1) Assault and Battery 傷害

Assault and battery are separate offenses. However, they often occur together, and that occurrence is referred to as "assault and battery". In an act of physical violence, assault refers to the act which causes the victim to apprehend imminent physical harm, while battery refers to the actual act causing the physical harm.

assault 與 battery 乃不同罪名，但常一起發生（此時稱為 assault and battery）。在暴行行為，assault 指引起被害人立即受到傷害之恐懼，而 battery 則指真正引起傷害之行為。*

* 故 battery 乃已完成之 assault，但現代制定法不分別這兩罪，而用 assault and battery 表示傷害行為。

(2) False Imprisonment 妨礙自由

It refers to one person forcibly restraining another person, against their will, with a risk of being seriously injured or killed. Any person who intentionally restricts another person's freedom or movement, without their consent, may be liable for false imprisonment.

指違反他人意願，強制扣留或拘束他人自由或行動，致有嚴重傷害或致死之虞。

(3) Kidnapping 擄人勒贖

Kidnapping is defined as the carrying away or confinement of a person by force or deception, without that person's consent. In other words, kidnapping is the seizure and detention of a person without their consent, while intending to carry away the person at a later time, hold the person for ransom, etc..

指未經同意，以暴力或騙術帶走或拘禁他人。易言之，未經同意，為了日後帶走或贖金等，扣留或拘禁他人。

(4) Homicide 殺人

It includes first and second degree murder, involuntary manslaughter, and vehicular homicide.

包括第一級與第二級謀殺，非自願殺人及車輛殺人。

(5) Rape 強姦

Also includes statutory rape and sexual assault.

包括法定強姦與性侵。

2. Property Crimes, or Offenses Against Property 財產犯罪

Property crimes involve interference with another person's right to use or enjoy their own property. Examples:

財產犯罪是妨害他人使用收益其財產之權利。例如：

(1) Larceny 竊盜

Refers to a type of theft in which a person takes another person's property and carries it away, with the intent to permanently deprive the legal owner of their property.

larceny 指意圖永久剝奪所有人之財產而取去其物。

(2) Robbery 強盜

It is known as theft by force, and may also be considered a personal crime as it often results in physical and mental harm.

指以暴力取去他人之物，也視爲一種人身犯罪，因常導致他人身心受創。

(3) Burglary 不法入室

It occurs when a person breaks and enters into a home or building, intending to commit a crime.

指意圖犯罪而闖入他人之房屋或建物。

(4) Arson 縱火

Arson is the willful and malicious burning or charring of another person's property or structure.

指故意與惡意焚毀他人之財產或不動產。

3. White Collar Crimes 白領犯罪

White Collar Crimes refers to financially motivated, nonviolent crimes committed by individuals, businesses and government professionals. They include:

指由個人、企業及政府專業人士基於財政動機所犯之非暴力犯罪。包含：

(1) Embezzlement 侵占

It refers to a type of white collar crime in which a person entrusted with the finances of another person or business illegally takes that money for their own personal use.

指一種白領犯罪，即受託處理他人或企業之財務，而不法將其金錢供自己使用。

(2) Forgery 僞造

It is another example of a white collar property crime, because it is the creation, alteration, forging, or imitation of any document with the intent to defraud another person of their property.

是另一種白領犯罪，意圖騙取別人財產，而創造、變造、僞造或仿造任何文書。

(3) False Pretenses 詐欺

False pretenses refers to a combination of fraud and larceny, in which a person misrepresents in order to obtain the property of another.

指詐騙與偷竊之合併，爲了取得他人之財產，爲不實之陳述。

(4) Receipt of Stolen Goods 收受贓物

It is a crime to receive or purchase property that you know or believe to be stolen, or otherwise obtained through theft.

指收受或購買明知或以爲偷竊之財產，或以他法經由竊盜而取得。

4. Organized Crime 組織犯罪

Organized crime is a continuing criminal enterprise that rationally works to profit from illicit activities that are often in great public demand.

是賡續性犯罪企業，自通常公共需求甚殷之違法活動獲取利潤。

5. High Tech Crime 高科技犯罪

Any crime that involves using a computer or network is generally referred to as a computer crime.

涉及使用電腦或網路之犯罪，一般稱爲電腦犯罪。

四、從犯之責任

When multiple parties are involved, people classify the participants as follows:

1. Principal in the first degree: those who actually commit a crime (i.e. the perpetrator). Perpetrators are not accomplices.

2. Principal in the second degree: those who aided, counseled, commanded, or encouraged the perpetrator in the actual commission of a crime. An abettor is considered an accomplice.[*]

3. Accessory[*] before the fact: those who aided, counseled, commanded, or encouraged the perpetrator to commit the crime, without actually being present at the moment of perpetration. An accessory (before the fact) is considered an accomplice.

4. Accessory after the fact: those who aid an individual, knowing the individual to be a criminal, in an effort to hinder individual's detection, arrest, trial, or punishment. Accessories (after the fact) are guilty of a separate crime.

當多人涉及犯罪時，將參與人區分如下：

1. 一級主犯：指眞正犯罪之人。犯人不是從犯。

2. 二級主犯：指協助、提供意見、命令或鼓勵犯人眞正從事犯罪之人。教唆人認爲從犯。

3. 事前從犯：指協助、提供意見、命令或鼓勵犯人犯罪之人。於犯罪時並未真正在場，被認為從犯。

4. 事後從犯：知悉犯人是犯罪，而加以協助，旨在妨害官署發現、逮捕、審理或處罰，這是犯了別的罪。

*accomplice 與 accessory 不同，accomplice 係於真正犯罪時在場，即使主犯不被追訴或定罪，亦可加以追訴。而 accessory 通常於犯罪時不在場，而可比 accomplice 或主犯受到較輕之刑罰。

To convict an accomplice, the prosecutor must prove that the accomplice acted in support of the perpetrator, and had the requisite mental state while doing so. Some states allow accomplices to be prosecuted independently of the principal perpetrator, so an accomplice could be found guilty of a more severe offense than the principal, or be convicted while the alleged perpetrator is acquitted.

檢方為使從犯定罪，須證明他協助主犯，且行為時具有所需之犯意。有些州准許從犯與主犯獨立追訴，致從犯可能判比主犯更重之罪，甚至主犯無罪而從犯卻被定罪。

（五）Sentencing Guidelines 處刑指南

Federal government and state governments have promulgated their various sentencing guidelines. Federal courts apply federal guidelines while state courts use state guidelines.*

聯邦政府與州政府為了避免法官量刑因人而異罰，訂了各種處刑指南，聯邦法院適用聯邦處刑指南，各州法院則使用該州的處刑指南。

*這些指南並非抽象的量刑規則，而是針對一罪量刑及數罪合併量刑作出具體明確的指導，使量刑較有可預測性，值得我國借鑑（我國刑法第57條雖訂有科刑審酌因素，但並未規定各因素如何評價及對量刑影響之程度。法官只要審酌該條各款情況而未逾越法定刑度，原則上不得指為違法）。

（六）No Ex Post Facto 法律不得溯及既往

Art. 1 of U.S. Constitution expressly prohibits a law that retroactively makes criminal conduct that was not criminal when performed.

美國憲法第1條明文禁止追溯處罰既往行爲之法律。

（七）No Punishment for Status 不可處罰身分

Law should not punish people just for their status. If any law does so, it is a cruel and unusual punishment, unconstitutional. For example, law should not punish homeless people, but may punish those who trespass or are vagrant.

任何制定法不得只因人的身分予以處罰，否則乃違反憲法之殘酷與不正常刑罰。例如法律不可處罰無家可歸之人，但可處罰他們闖入私地或閒蕩之行爲。

（八）Defenses 抗辯

Many defenses are available for the accused:

被告對刑事訴追有很多抗辯：

1. Failure of Proof 欠缺證據

The prosecution has not or cannot prove an element of the offense.

檢方尚未或無法證明犯罪之要件。

2. Mistakes 錯誤

In certain circumstances, an individual's mistake can be used as a defense.

(1) Mistake of Law: a mistake regarding the legal status or effect of some situation. Ignorance of the law is no defense.

(2) Mistake of Fact: a mistake regarding the facts of some situation.

錯誤有時可作爲抗辯。

(1) 法律錯誤：指對若干情況之法律地位或效果之錯誤，但不知法律，並不能作爲抗辯理由。

(2) 事實錯誤：對若干情況事實之錯誤。

3. Justifications 免責事由

When an act is justified, a person is not criminally liable even though their act would otherwise constitute an offense. These are complete defenses:

當一行爲符合法定要件時，即使該行爲原來構成犯罪，亦可不負刑事責任。這是完全抗辯，包括：

(1) Self-Defense: the use of force to protect oneself from an attempted injury by another.

(A) Defense of property: a person may use force to protect his property from a felony occurring within.

(B) Defense of Others: the right of a person to protect a third party with reasonable force against an assailant who seeks to inflict force upon the third party.

(1) 自衛：使用暴力防護自己免於他人之傷害

(A) 防衛財產：使用暴力防護其財產免於他人重罪之發生。

(B) 防衛他人：使用合理力量，防護第三人免於他人之攻擊。

(2) Necessity 緊急避難

Sometimes referred to as the "choice of evils", the necessity defense allows an individual to engage in otherwise unlawful conduct if by doing so the individual avoids a greater harm.

緊急避難有時稱爲惡害之抉擇。即准許行爲人爲了避免更大損害，所從事之本來不法行爲。

4. Excuses 可宥恕事由

A type of defense that exempts the accused from liability because of certain circumstance, but does not actually condone the result (at least in part) of his actions. They are partial defenses:

(1) Duress: actions may sometimes be excused if the actor is able to establish a defense called duress. The defense can arise when there's a threat or actual use of physical force that drives the defendant to commit a crime.

(2) Intoxication: involuntary intoxication can be a defense to criminal charges if it prevents the defendant from forming the intent that is required.

(3) Insanity: criminal insanity is a mental defect or disease that makes it impossible for a defendant to understand their actions, or to understand that their actions are wrong.

指由於若干情況，免除被告之責任之抗辯，但不真正（至少一部）宥恕被告行為結果之責任，這些是部分抗辯，*包括：

(1) 脅迫：如行為人能證明具有脅迫之抗辯時，有時可阻卻行為責任。如受到威脅或真正使用物理力量，驅使被告犯罪時，可發生此種抗辯。

(2) 酗酒：非自願酒醉，如導致被告無法形成所需之犯意，則可作為各種刑事追訴之抗辯。

(3) 精神失常：精神失常是一種精神缺陷或病態，致被告無法了解其行為或了解其行為是不對。**

*完全抗辯與部分抗辯之區別在於前者阻卻違法，不成立犯罪，後者成立犯罪，但可能阻卻刑責，即可能減輕其刑。

**精神病人通常由於不能形成必需之犯意，因此不能認為有罪。

補充：

Roe v. Wade, 410 U.S. 113, was a landmark decision of the U.S. Supreme Court in 1973 in which the Court ruled that the Constitution of the United States generally protects a pregnant woman's liberty to choose to have an abortion. But the Supreme Court overturned Roe v. Wade this June, allowing states to determine abortion access, creating lots of controversy and criticism.

羅訴韋德案（Roe v. Wade），為聯邦最高法院於1973年對於婦女墮胎權以及隱私權之重要案例，承認婦女的墮胎權，受到憲法隱私權的保護。但去年6月該法院推翻羅訴韋德案，此後關於女性是否允許墮胎的問題，將交由各州自行決定，引起各方震驚與撻伐。

（注）本文參考

1. Criminal Law
   https://www.law.cornell.edu/wex/criminal_law
2. Weinerman, Practical Law, A Layperson's Handbook (Prenticehall,1978).
3. https://www.stimmel-law.com/en/articles/american-system-criminal-justice
4. 楊崇森，遨遊美國法，第一冊第八章，美國刑法之原理與運用，頁307以下。

二、詞彙

mala in se：自然犯

mala prohibita：法定犯

common law crimes：普通法犯罪

Penal Code：刑法典

mens rea：犯意

presumption of innocence：推定無辜

ex post facto：追溯既往

due process of law：正當法律程序

preempt：獨占

infractions：違規

petty offense：微罪

public welfare offenses：公共福利犯罪

vicarious liability：代理責任

proximate causation：相當因果關係

proximate：相當因果

intervening cause：外在介入原因

felonies：重罪

misdemeanors：輕罪

inchoate offenses：不完整之犯罪（包括未遂、通謀與教唆）

preliminary crime：初步犯罪、不完整犯罪

strict liability offenses：負絕對責任之罪

white color crime：白領犯罪

cyber and computer crimes：電腦犯罪

wire fraud：網路詐欺

identity theft：竊用他人身分

organized crimes：組織犯罪

hate crimes：憎恨罪

whistle blower：檢舉同事不法行為之人（吹哨者）

driving while intoxicated：酒醉駕車

venue：審判地

intent：故意

general intent：一般故意

specific intent：特定故意

doctrine of transferred intent：移轉犯意之原則

recklessness：不在意

knowingly：知情

attempted crimes：未遂犯

attempted robbery：強盜未遂

attempt：未遂

principal：主犯

solicitation：教唆

abettor：教唆人

conspiracy：通謀

accessory：從犯

accomplice：從犯

complicity：共犯

aider：幫助犯

lookout：把風

scene：現場

proximate cause：相當因果關係

commission：犯了罪

state-specific：特定州

Sentencing Guidelines：量刑指南

infancy：未成年人

defense of entrapment：陷阱抗辯

justifications：合法事由（免責事由）

defense：抗辯、免責事由

self defense：正當防衛

defense of others：防衛他人

defense of property：防衛財產

insanity：精神失常

duress：脅迫

intoxication：酗酒

necessity：緊急避難

coercion：強制

mistake：錯誤

consent：同意

condon：宥恕

provocation：被挑釁

infraction：微罪（如交通違規）

capital crime：可判死刑之罪

genocide：種族滅絕

espionage：間諜

treason：叛亂

sedition：煽動騷亂

riot：暴動

sabotage：破壞、抵制

kidnapping：綁票、擄人勒贖

abduction：綁架

extortion：勒索

blackmail：恐嚇取財

perjury：偽證

escape：脫逃

contempt of court：藐視法庭

misprision of felony：隱匿重罪犯

forgery：偽造文書

counterfeiting：偽造貨幣

bribery：賄賂

interference with a juror：干擾陪審員

obstruction of justice：妨害司法

disturbing the piece：妨礙治安

criminal trespass：刑事侵入住宅

vagrancy：遊蕩、遊民

homicile：殺人

murder：謀殺

manslaughter：過失殺人、誤殺

voluntary manslaughter：有意殺人

involuntary manslaughter：無意殺人

mayhem：傷害肢體、重傷

assault and battery：傷害、毆打

bigamy：重婚

adultery：通姦

rape：強姦

statutory rape：法定強姦

seduction：誘姦

abortion：墮胎

sodomy：獸姦

child sexual abuse：對兒童之性虐待

domestic violence：家暴

false imprisonment：妨害自由

Breach of prison：越獄

forcible entry and detainer：侵入住宅

stalking：跟蹤

defamation：妨害名譽

libel：以出版品誹謗

slander：言詞誹謗

arson：縱火

vandalism：毀損

larceny / burglary：竊盜

robbery：強盜

receiving stolen property ：收受贓物

abuse of trust crimes：濫用信任之犯罪

obtaining property by false pretenses：詐欺取財

embezzlement：侵占

money laundering：洗錢

narcotics trafficking：販毒

trespassing：非法侵入

loitering：遊蕩

shoplifting：店內扒竊

pardon：赦免

diversion：換刑

probation：緩刑

restitution：賠償

conviction：定罪

indeterminate sentence：不定期刑

parole：假釋

commit to：送入（監所、感化院）

clemency：赦免

commutation：減刑

第二節　我國法

特色

1. Our law does not have obstruction of justice crime.
   無妨害司法罪。

2. No separate conspiracy crime.
   無通謀罪。

3. Our law does not have the classification of felony and misdemeanor as the U.S.

無重罪與輕罪之分。

4. The abetter and the principal are subject to the same penalty.

教唆犯與正犯同罰。

5. There is no contempt of court crime.

無蔑視法庭罪。

6. The penalty of the accused who are over eighty of age can be reduced.

老髦減刑。

7. The penalty of those accused who voluntarily surrender to the authority may be reduced.

自首得減。

8. Those crimes based upon certain relationship (such as theft or murder, assault and battery between relatives) may be reduced or exempted from criminal liability.

因一定親屬關係而成立之犯罪（親屬相盜、殺傷等）可能減免。

9. We have not promulgated sentencing guidelines.

尚無量刑指南。

10. We have some kind of witness and victim protection system.

已有初步保障證人與犯罪被害人制度。

11. We have different kinds of rehabilitative measures.

有各種保安處分。

12. We do not have indeterminate imprisonment systems.

尚無不定期刑。

13. We have decriminalized adultery crime.

通姦（adultery）已除罪。

14. We do not punish vagrancy crime.

無遊蕩罪。

15. We do not punish hate crimes.

無懷恨罪。

第三節　習題

選擇題（四選一）

1. A bought from B a jewel which he knew was stolen from a shop. A is guilty of _____.

   (1) contempt of court

   (2) tort

   (3) receipt of stolen goods

   (4) larceny

2. A agreed with B to kidnap C but never carry it out. A commits_____.

   (1) a conspiracy

   (2) no crime

   (3) misdemeanor

   (4) petit crime

3. A, a salesman, promised to provide certain goods for B, but he delivered a counterfeiting one. A is guilty of_____.

   (1) larceny

   (2) false pretense

   (3) embezzlement

   (4) conspiracy

4. In the U.S., anybody may as a rule use necessary force to protect himself against an apparent threat of unlawful and direct attack from another. It is called _____.

(1) necessity

(2) self defense

(3) private necessity

(4) excuse

5. An attorney, used the funds in an escrow account for himself. He is guilty of_____.

(1) conversion

(2) felony

(3) embezzlement

(4) fraud

6. Those when he commits a crime is insane, while not to constitute a crime, will be remit to _____ as long as his insanity lasts.

(1) a hospital

(2) a court

(3) a school

(4) a experimental organization

7. A persuaded B to kill C by feeding him certain poison. B did not go ahead. A is guilty of _____.

(1) solicitation

(2) no crime

(3) at temptation

(4) conspiracy

8. In the above case, B is guilty of _____.

(1) no crime

(2) manslaughter

(3) conspiracy

(4) attempted murder

9. A confined B for two days in an attempt to extort money from B. A is guilty of _____.

    (1) theft

    (2) robbery

    (3) false pretense

    (4) kidnapping

10. A forced B to cheat money from C. So B did as ordered. B can argued that he is not guilty because _____.

    (1) he was under duress

    (2) he was cheated

    (3) he was innocent

    (4) he has a necessity

11. _____ (like shoplifting) usually punished by a fine of no more than $1000 and no more than one year of imprisonment in a jail.

    (1) Manslaughter

    (2) Petit crime

    (3) Misdemeanor

    (4) Traffic violation

12. A, a firefighter, tore down B's house next to C's house which was on fire. A's act is _____.

    (1) a private necessity

    (2) a public necessity

    (3) a trespass

    (4) a nuisance

13. A, B's attorney, concealed certain money which he should retuned to B. A is guilty of _____.

    (1) malpractice

    (2) conversion

    (3) felony

    (4) fraud

14. _____ is a conditional release from prison and the man is overseen by the states correctional system.

(1) Community service

(2) Probation

(3) Parole

(4) House arrest

15. Dissuade a person from testifying is guilty of the crime of _____ .

(1) obstruction of justice

(2) contempt of court

(3) disturbing the peace

(4) vagrancy

16. An act that is disrespectful to the court process may constitute the crime of _____ .

(1) no crime

(2) obstruction of justice

(3) contempt of court

(4) disturbing the piece

17. Tampering with a witness, victim, or an informant may constitute crime of _____ .

(1) obstruction of justice

(2) obstruction of public affairs

(3) obstruction of freedom

(4) perjury

18. In U.S., some states provide program of _____ for crime victim & witness.

(1) protection

(2) encouragement of disclosing crime

(3) whistle blower

(4) crime prevention

19. Money laundering is a kind of _____.

    (1) mala prohibita

    (2) against personal crime

    (3) against property crime

    (4) organized crime

20. An assault is like a / an _____, while a battery is like a completed assault.

    (1) attempted battery

    (2) fight

    (3) battery

    (4) inchoate offenses

21. Sedition is close to _____ in that both crimes are concerned with social order.

    (1) vagrancy

    (2) theft

    (3) vandalism

    (4) treason

22. Federal courts and some states in U.S. have _____ for judges to apply in rendering the penalty.

    (1) Sentencing Guidelines

    (2) statute

    (3) criteria

    (4) no criteria

23. _____ means the penalty may be decreased.

    (1) Diversion

    (2) Probation

    (3) Commutation

    (4) Parole

24. Accessory and accomplice means they are not _____.

    (1) principal

    (2) criminal

    (3) defendant

    (4) accused

25. Defamation consist of libel and_____.

    (1) stalking

    (2) theft

    (3) assault

    (4) slander

26. Vandalism is somewhat similar to _____, in that both belong to crime against property.

    (1) arson

    (2) perjury

    (3) force imprisonment

    (4) defamation

27. The penalty of committing _____ is very severe.

    (1) larceny

    (2) treason

    (3) obstruction of justice

    (4) shoplifting

▲選擇題解答

1. (3)　2. (1)　3. (2)　4. (2)　5. (3)　6. (1)　7. (1)　8. (2)　9. (4)

10. (1)　11. (3)　12. (2)　13. (2)　14. (3)　15. (1)　16. (3)　17. (1)　18. (1)

19. (4)　20. (1)　21. (4)　22. (1)　23. (4)　24. (1)　25. (4)　26. (1)　27. (2)

第四節　詞彙整理

一、同義或類似詞

divide－distribute

legal－legitimate

testify－testimony－deposition

verify－proof－notarize－void－
　voidable

argue－support－maintain－initiate

deem－presume

deed－document

doubt－dissent

case－event－situation－
　circumstance

crime－offend

conform－meet－satisfy－observe－
　follow

criminal－accused－offender

aid－abet－advise－encourage－
　suggest－move

revenge－return

punish－penalize

parole－pardon－amnesty

act－action－movement

need－require－demand－order－
　rule

restore－return－status quo

equity－fair－justice

partner－associate

affiliate－subsidiary

court－tribunal

crime－criminal－perpetrators

amend－amendment－revise－
　change－modify

void－voidable－invalid－
　ineffective－unenforceable

terminate－dissolve－finish－
　rescind－recall－annul

effective－enforceable－operative－
　active

file－submit－bring

settlement－compromise－
　arbitration－conciliation

suit－litigation

conclude－enter into－sign

contract－agreement－gentleman's
　agreement－memorandum of
　understanding

conference－meeting－treaty

unconscionable－unethical

confidential－non-disclosure

confer－entitle－entrust－give－
　grant

ask－demand－petition－apply－
application

permit－permission－approve－
approval－agree－consent－
accept

decide－adjudicate－determine

honest－reliable－reasonable－
trustworthy－trust－reliance

summon－subpoena

wording－language

proof－evidence－prove－testimony

clause－proviso－provision－article

title－ownership－possession－
belong to－belonging

transfer－deliver

term－condition－contingency

compensate－indemnification

exchange－qui-pro-quo

gift－donate

excuse－justification

judge－adjudicator－arbiter－
assessor

supervise－oversee

estate－real estate－intangible estate

tangible estate－personal estate

credit－creditor

bankruptcy－bankrupt

affidavit－document－license－
certificate

二、反義詞

affirmative; negative

cause; effect

opponent; proponent; supporter

express; implied

writing; written; oral

(relative) collateral; lineal

三、詞性轉換

（一）動詞 → 名詞

prosecute → prosecution

protect → protection

punish → punishment

state → statement

warn → warning

perform → performance

terminate → termination

admit → admission

compensate → compensation

cause → causation

base → basis

assert → assertion

accuse → accused → accusation

attach → attachment

argue → argument

act → action

allege → allegation

admit → admission

encourage → encouragement

incriminate → incrimination

indict → indictment

inform → information

injure → injury

examine → examination

instruct → instruction

try → trial → hearing

deprive → deprivation

disturb → disturbance

deter → deterrence

fail → failure

break → breach

forge → forgery

guide → guidance

appear → appearance

commit → commitment

consider → consideration

seize → seizure

serve → service

separate → separation

differ → difference

deter → deterrence

notarize → notary

object → objection

intent → intention

interpret → interpretation

intervene → intervention

interrogate → interrogation

judge → judgment

suspend → suspension

suspect → suspicion

sue → suit

explain → explanation

arbitrate → arbitration

arrest → apprehension

conspire → conspiracy

plead → pleading → process

acquit → acquittal

confess → confession

（二）名詞 → 動詞或副詞

effect → effective

enforce → enforceable

equality → equal

condition → conditional

innocence → innocent

deceive → deceptive

consequence → consequent →
consequential

liability → liable

contingency → contingent

part → partial

pay → payment → payable

majority → major

penalty → penal

minority → minor

guilt → guilty

（三）動詞 → 身分類名詞

offend → offender

appeal → appellant → appellee →
respondent

debt → debtor

credit → creditor

parole → parolee

trespass → trespasser

defend → defender → public
defender

defense → defender

guarantee → guarantor

第七章　公司法

第一節　美國法

一、介紹

A corporation can be created by a single or multiple shareholders and formed as a for-profit or a not-for-profit entity. Most corporations are for profit.

美國公司係由一個或眾多股東所設立。分為營利或非營利組織。大多數公司為營利法人。

Corporations can enter into contracts, sue and be sued, own assets and borrow money from financial institutions.

公司可締結契約、控告他人或被告、擁有資產、向金融機構借款。

The creation of a corporation needs a process called incorporation where articles of incorporation (articles or charter) contains the purpose of the business, name and location, and the number of shares and types of stock issued. Thus protects its owners from being personally liable in the event of a lawsuit. After charter is filed, shareholders are to elect directors, appoint officers and adopt bylaws.

公司之設立需經一套設立之法律程序，即起草章程，涵蓋營業之目的、名稱與地點，發行之股份數額與股份種類。因此可保護股東在涉訟時不必自己負責。在章程呈報主管機關後，由股東選出董事與通過符合章程之細則（bylaws*）。

*bylaws 係訂定公司業務執行之規定。

Anyone who acted on behalf of an unformed corporation is personally liable for the obligations incurred. He may later reimburse from the corporation.

發起人（promoter）之責任：為未成立之公司與人交易之發起人，由其個人對債權人負責。但日後可向公司報銷。

二、特色

1. The common form of corporation are C corporation and S corporation.

   一般公司多是C公司與S公司。

2. The U.S. can have one person companies.

   有一人公司。

3. Unlike the corporation law in Taiwan, American law does not have supervisor.

   不似我公司法，並不設監察人。

4. In Many states in the U.S. the board members are not necessarily their shareholders.

   很多州董事不必限於股東。

5. Directors owe fiduciary duty towards their shareholders.

   董事對股東有信任義務（fiduciary duty）。

6. Shareholders may sometimes bring derivative suit against the executives and management of the company.

   股東有時可提起傳來訴訟。

7. Anti-trust law is well developed. However the trend has seen great reversal in the last several decades. There are more and more corporate mergers and acquisition and consolidation of corporate power.

   反托拉斯法發達，但近年來趨勢已有逆轉，愈來愈多公司進行併購。

8. They have authorized capital, no-par stock and voting trust.

有授權資本制、無面額股份、表決權信託。

9. Sometimes the corporate veil may be pierced.

有時可揭開公司面紗。

10. Election of directors may use cumulative voting.

董事選舉可行累積投票制。

11. They have both public and close corporation.

有公眾持有與封閉型公司（public and close corporation）之分。

12. They have corporate reorganization system.

有公司重整制度。

13. In recent years limit liability companies (LLC) have become popular.

近年來有有限責任公司（甚至一人公司）出現。

14. In most states there are Blue Sky Laws regulating securities market.

大多數州有青天法規範證券買賣。

15. In recent years corporate merger and acquisition have become more common.

近年流行公司併購。

16. 公法人亦稱爲Public corporation。

三、公司主要分類

（一）C Corporation C 公司

C Corporation is the most common form. Owners receive profits and are taxed at the individual level, while the corporation itself is taxed as a business entity.

C 公司是美國最常見之公司形態。股東領取盈餘，由個人付稅，而公司本身則作爲商業法人課稅。

（二）S Corporation S 公司

S Corporation is created in the same way as a C Corporation but is different in owner limitation and tax purposes. It consists of up to 100 shareholders, the profits/losses are borne by the shareholders.

S 公司之設立方式與 C 公司相同，但股東有人數限制，且課稅之目的不同。S 公司由股東一百人以下組成，公司之盈虧由股東負擔。

四、優點和缺點

（一）Advantages 優點

1. Separate legal entity.
   獨立法人。
2. Unlimited life.
   存續期間無限。
3. Limited liability: Company owners are only liable for the amount they invested. Creditors have no claim to the owners' personal assets for payments owed by the shareholders.
   有限責任：公司股東只負責自己投資之數額，債權人對股東個人所欠公司之資產，並無請求權。
4. Easy transfer of ownership shares: Stocks can be easily traded in the market.
   移轉股權容易：出售個人之股份或股票時，容易在市場交易。
5. Limited liability.
   有限責任。
6. Source of capital: Corporations can derive funds from selling stocks and issuing bonds.
   資本來源：公司可出賣股份、發行債券而取得資金。

（二）Disadvantages 缺點

Double taxation and documentation.
雙重稅捐、應呈報年度報告、製作會計紀錄。

五、介紹

（一）Shareholder and Shareholders' Meeting 股東與股東會

1. Shareholder 股東*
*股東對公司日常營運無經營權。

Shareholder owes no fiduciary or loyalty duty to the corporation or other shareholders.

股東對公司或他股東不負信任或忠實義務。

Piercing the corporate veil: When the shareholders treat corporate assets as their own, fail to observe formalities and result injustice, the court may disregard a corporate entity and hold individuals liable for corporate obligations.

揭開公司面紗：當公司股東將公司資產當作自己的資產，或怠於遵守公司手續，或有詐欺等導致不公正結果時，美國法院可能不顧公司之形式而要求該股東個人負責公司之債務。

2. Shareholders' Meeting 股東會

Corporation must hold annual shareholders' meeting. Special shareholders' meeting may be called by the board of directors, the holders of 1/10 or more of all shares. Shareholder may vote in person or by proxy.

股東會分為常會與臨時會，常會應每年召開。臨時會可由董事會或超過十分之一以上股份之股東召開*。股東可親自或託人代理出席股東大會投票。
*股東大會之開會日須依法預先通知。

Proxy solicitation should disclose all material facts about proposals to be voted and no fraud, etc..

股東會委託書須由公司透露所有有關表決事項之重要事實，禁止失誤、省略或詐欺等。

Voting trust: All shares own by the parties are transferred to a trustee, who votes the shares and distributes the dividends pursuant to the agreement to those shareholders.

表決權信託：乃一種股東書面約定，將所有股份移轉給某一受託人，由受託人行使表決權，並依該約定分配盈餘予各股東。*

*須將一份信託契約與信託受益人之姓名與地址向公司呈報。信託期間限十年。

Cumulative voting: Articles may provide for cumulative voting, in which each shareholder can vote equal to the numbers of his shares multiplied by the numbers of directors to be elected with the total number divided among the candidates.

累積投票制：章程可規定每個股東可按其股數乘上要選董事之人數，投票予一個或數個候選人。

Derivative action: one or more shareholders bring an action in the name of the corporation against a party or parties causing harm to the latter. Recovery goes to the corporation and not to the shareholder(s). Basically the shareholder should first demand the corporation to bring the suit.

傳來訴訟：股東以公司名義對侵害公司之人起訴*，訴訟結果歸公司而非股東。原則上須先書面請求公司起訴。

*如董事會怠於起訴才可提出。如訴訟結果有益於公司時，法院於訴訟結束時，可命公司支付該股東付出之合理費用。

（二）Board of Directors 董事會

A corporation consists of a board of directors elected by

shareholders. Each shareholder has one vote per share. Shareholders can be elected as the board members.

公司成立董事會，董事由股東選出。股東原則上每股一票，可被選為公司董事。

The board of directors make decisions on major issues and policies of the corporation. They owe a duty of care to the shareholders, and act in the best interests of the shareholders and the corporation.

董事會決定公司之重大問題與政策，對股東負注意義務，為股東與公司之最佳利益而行動。

Directors need not be shareholders. Director owes duty of loyalty and duty of care that ordinarily prudent person exercise in a like position.

董事不必限於股東，負善良管理人之注意義務。

Conflicting interest transaction should be disclosed to and approved by the board or shareholders. Otherwise it may be set aside or liable for the damages, except it is fair to the corporation.

利益衝突之交易，董事須向董事會或股東透露並取得同意，否則除對公司公平外，其交易可被撤銷或要求賠償與董事所得利益相同之損害。

（三）Issuance of Stock 發行股票

The issuance or trading of stock must comply with state law and federal securities law. Stocks are common stock and special stock, par value and no-par stocks.

有關股票之發行或出售須遵照美國各州法令與聯邦證券交易法。股票分為普通股及特別股，有面額股及無面額股。

（四）Dissolution and Liquidation 解散與清算

When the term of a corporation expires or becomes bankrupt, it must go through liquidation facilitated by a liquidator. The corporate assets will be sold and the proceeds go to creditors to pay off debt, then given to shareholders. Involuntary liquidation is usually triggered by creditors of an insolvent or bankrupt company.

當公司存續期間屆滿或破產時，應經清算程序（由清算人負責）。即出售公司資產，將賣得價款給債權人還債，賸餘則分給股東。非自願之清算多由無清償能力或破產公司之債權人所發動。

（五）Popular States for Foreign Corporations 受外國人歡迎之州

For foreign corporations incorporating in U.S., the most popular states are California, Delaware and New York because their laws are more flexible.

外國公司在美國設立公司，最受歡迎的是加利福尼亞州、德拉瓦州及紐約州，因這三州法令較為靈活。

（六）Limited Liability Company (LLC) 有限責任公司

It is popular nowadays because it blends elements of partnership and corporation, provides limited liability as a corporation, but easier to form and operate. It needs not to have officers and directors, board or shareholder meetings, or other administrative burdens as a corporation. Many LLCs have only one member. Certain professional business such as legal or medical services, may not form an LLC but use a Professional Limited Liability Company (PLLC).

有限責任公司兼有合夥與公司之長*，晚近受到歡迎。有限公司只負有限責任，但容易成立運作。不需公司之職員、董事、董事會或其他行政負擔。許多有限責任公司只有一個成員。銀行、信託、保險，禁止用 LLC 公司形式。專業人員如法律、醫療，不能組成 LLC，而須用專業有限責任公司名義。

＊如合夥般抽稅，股東可轉讓權利，但經營權除外。

（七）Merger and Acquisition 公司之併購

Fundamental changes in corporate structure needs: (1)The board adopts a resolution, (2)written notice is given to shareholders, (3) shareholders approve by a majority votes, (4) amended article filed with the state.

公司重大改變須經下列程序：(1)董事會通過；(2)書面通知股東；(3)有權投票之股東過半數同意（須經股東全部投票權之過半數，而非股東會決議之出席人所投票數之過半數）；(4)將章程變更呈報州政府。

Dissenting shareholder may ask the corporation to purchase his shares.

不同意公司重大變更之股東可請求公司買取其股份。

A merger means two separate corporations combine to form a new one and a acquisition denotes the takeover, of one corporation by another. M&A can be friendly or hostile, depending on the approval of the target company's board. Hostile takeover means a company or group of investors attempts to acquire a publicly traded company against the wishes of its upper management. Hostile takeovers are perfectly legal.

併購分爲合併與收購兩種。前者係由兩家（以上）規模相當的企業合併爲一家公司，而後者指由一家公司收購另一公司的股票或資產。按是否取得目標公司董事會同意，可分爲敵意收購與善意收購二種。敵意併購乃指公司取得公開上市公司，而不顧其管理高層意願之謂。敵意併購完全合法。

Motives for mergers: cost reduction or higher revenues, higher growth, stronger market power.

併購之動機包含減少支出、提高收入、加速成長及取得更大市場力量。

（注）本文參考：

1. 6 types of corporations: Which is right for your startup? https://www.brex.com/blog/types-of-corporations/
2. https://kknews.cc/finance/jre5apl.html
3. https://iclg.com/practice-areas/corporate-governance-laws-and-regulations/usa
4. The Essential Corporate Law in the United States (USA) https://www.ilpabogados.com/en/the-essential-corporate-law-in-the-united-states-usa/

六、詞彙

legal entity：法人

stockholder / shareholders：股東

remit federal and state taxes：繳納聯邦與州稅捐

incorporation：設立公司

shares / stock：股份

issued：發行

day-to-day running：日常營運

board of directors：董事會

duty of care：注意義務

enter into：締結

charter：章程

regardless of：不問……

limited liability：有限責任

easy transfer：易於移轉

liquidated(v.) / liquidation(n.)：清算

selling stocks and issuing bonds：出售股份與發行債券

dissolve：解散

liquidator：清算人

involuntary liquidation：非自願清算

corporate assets：公司資產

proceeds：收益

insolvent or bankrupt company：清償不能或破產公司

merger and acquisition：合併與收購

hostile and friendly takeover：惡意與善意合併

join stock：合股公司

treasury stock：庫藏股

unissued stock：未發行股份

par stock：面額股

no-par stock：無面額股

par value：面額

dividend：盈餘

subsidiary company：子公司

affiliated company：關係企業

charter：公司章程

bylaws：公司辦事細則

statutes：制定法

unincorporated society：非法人團體

partnership：合夥

duration：存續期間

public, municipal, private corporation：公共、市、私人公司

natural person：自然人

separate and distinct entity：獨立法律上個體

incorporate：組織公司

withdrawal：撤回

disability：無行為能力

charter：章程

stockholder：股東

immune：免責

cooperative：合作社

foreign corporation：外國公司

domestic corporation：國內公司

articles of incorporation：章程細則

certificate of incorporation：公司註冊證書

paid-in capital：已繳資本

directors：董事

officers：高級職員

agents：代理人

treasurer：財務長

president：董事長

secretary：秘書長

chief executive officer：簡稱CEO，台灣稱為執行長，是公司最高經營管理人，負責決策、發號施令，並承擔經營成果，對董事會負責。有的董事會派董事長擔任，能為董事帳暨執行長（chairmen & CEO），有的由總經理（president / managing director）出任，稱為president & CEO。CEO職稱在歐美較為常見，國內通常無此職務，有的亂用，例如將CEO置於總經理之下，而總經理之上有真正管事的董事長

duration：期間

subscribe：認股

board members：董事

proceeding of shareholders (regular or special)：股東會（經常或特別）

in the best interests of：為謀……之最佳利益

removed：解任

set forth：規定

specify：限定

promoter：發起人

share option：股份選擇權

profit-sharing：分享利益

associate：幫辦

discretionary：有裁量權的

majority vote：多數股票

fiduciary relation：信賴關係

discharge duties：踐履職務

in good faith：善意

vacancy：出缺

dissolution：解散

incur liability：負擔債務

bonds：債券

corporate name：公司名稱

vested interest：既得權

right to information：知之權利

inspect：檢閱

books and records：簿冊

proceedings of the stockholders：股東會議

proceedings of the directors：董事會議

in person or by proxy：親自或代理

calendar year：曆年

cumulative voting：累積投票制

voting trust：表決權信託

trustee：受託人

certificate of stock：股票

common stock：普通股

guaranteed stock share：保證股份

transferable：可轉讓的

fiction：擬制

pierced the corporate veil：揭開公司面紗透視其結構

capitalization：資本總額

capital stock：股本

treasury stock：庫藏股

unissued stock：未發行股份

profits：盈利

insolvent：支付不能

deadlock：僵局

exceed or abuse：越權或濫用

procured：取得

annual report：年報

franchise tax：特許稅

attorney general：檢察長

receiver：破產公司之管理人

registered agent：登記之代理人

equity suit：衡平法上訴訟

mismanagement：管理不善

decree：命令

interested party：利害關係人

distribution：分配

issuance：發行

institute proceeding：起訴

appraiser：評價人

terms and conditions：條款

anti-trust laws：反托拉斯法

wind up：結束

surviving corporation：殘存公司

merger：新設合併

consolidation：吸收合併

subsidiary company：子公司

affiliated company：關係企業

第二節　我國法

特色

1. No cumulative voting, no piercing corporate veil, no no-par stock.
   無累積投票制，無揭開公司面紗，無無面額股。

2. We have one person company now.
   有一人公司。

3. Board members can only be shareholders.
   董事限於股東。

4. Whether directors owe fiduciary duty towards shareholders is not clear.
   董事似不對股東負信任義務（fiduciary duty）。

5. Whether voting trust is recognized is not clear.
   無表決權信託，待考。

6. We have unlimited companies with limited liability shareholders.
   有兩合公司。

第三節　習題

選擇題（四選一）

1. Aside from charter, a document, ie., _____ is needed in formation of corporation.
   - (1) article of incorporation
   - (2) name of creditor
   - (3) credit record
   - (4) birth certificate

2. Any Corporation must file _____ to the government agency in charge.
   - (1) annual reports
   - (2) proceeding
   - (3) tax returns
   - (4) crime reports

3. Banks or insurance companies cannot form as a _____.
   - (1) S corporation
   - (2) C corporation
   - (3) limited liability company
   - (4) charitable entity

4. In some states, some types of _____ cannot form an ordinary corporation or an LLC.
   - (1) professionals
   - (2) accused
   - (3) judges
   - (4) bank

5. Many _____ have only one member with no maximum limit.

    (1) limited liability company

    (2) sole proprietor

    (3) public corporation

    (4) close corporation

6. Different from corporation, a _____ is personally liable for all business debts and lawsuits.

    (1) sole proprietor

    (2) charitable entity

    (3) limited corporation

    (4) investment advisor

7. _____ is a relatively new business structure and more suitable for running small business.

    (1) Limited Liability Company

    (2) Affiliated company

    (3) Parent company

    (4) Stock corporation

8. Not-for-profit entities operate under the category of _____.

    (1) scientific organization

    (2) vocational organization

    (3) charitable organization

    (4) educational organization

9. In U.S. many corporations issue a stock called "_____" aside from ordinary stock.

    (1) no-par stock

    (2) par stock

    (3) bond

    (4) certificate

10. Sometimes the court may investigate the structure of its shareholders and treat the rights or duties of a corporation as the rights or liabilities of its shareholders, based on the theory of "___ ___".

    (1) fiduciary duty

    (2) assumption of risk

    (3) piercing the corporate veil

    (4) illegal intention

11. In order to participate in the management of corporation,the minority shareholders can use the system of _____ to enter the board of directors.

    (1) cumulative voting

    (2) absent voting

    (3) plural voting

    (4) single voting

12. In many states of U.S., the directors of a corporation are _____ their shareholders.

    (1) not limited to

    (2) necessary

    (3) limited

    (4) exclusively

13. In U.S., _____ is often used by minority shareholders to gain seats in the board of directors.

    (1) voting trust

    (2) anti-trust

    (3) voting

    (4) derivative suit

14. Recently in order to enlarge their influence, _____ of corporations are in the increase.

    (1) mergers and acquisitions

    (2) acquisition

    (3) bankruptcy

    (4) decrease of capital

15. Most states in U.S. have so-called " _____ law" to regulate securities trade.

    (1) green sky

    (2) white sky

    (3) blue sky

    (4) sunny sky

16. Stocks or shares of every kind of corporation can be _____ traded in the market.

    (1) easily

    (2) difficultly

    (3) sometimes

    (4) generally

17. When a corporation is wind up, it shall go through a procedure called _____.

    (1) bankruptcy

    (2) dissolution

    (3) liquidation

    (4) reorganization

18. Under certain circumstances, a shareholder can on behalf of the corporation bring an action against a director, called _____.

    (1) derivative suit

    (2) indirect suit

    (3) direct suit

    (4) primary suit

19. Treasury stock, also known as reacquired stock, refers to previously _____ that is bought back from stockholders by the issuing company.
    (1) common stock
    (2) preferred stock
    (3) outstanding stock
    (4) par stock

20. A subsidiary is a company whose parent company is a majority shareholder that owns more than 50% of all the subsidiary company's shares. Affiliate is used to describe a company with a parent company that only possesses less than _____ in the ownership of the affiliate.
    (1) few
    (2) minority stake
    (3) majority
    (4) half

▲選擇題解答

1. (1)	2. (1)	3. (1)	4. (1)	5. (1)	6. (1)	7. (1)	8. (3)	9. (1)
10. (3)	11. (1)	12. (1)	13. (1)	14. (1)	15. (3)	16. (1)	17. (3)	18. (1)
19. (3)	20. (4)							

第四節　詞彙整理

一、類似詞

company－corporation

exceed－abuse

profit－dividend

charter－bylaws

affiliated－subsidiary

separate－distinct

fiduciary－fiducial

set forth－provide－specify

institute proceeding－bring an action

二、反義詞

insolvent; solvent

minority; majority

preferred stock; common stock

par value; no par stock

public corporation; close corporation

common stock; preferred stock

temporary; ordinary

三、詞性轉換

（一）動詞 → 名詞

incorporate → incorporation

bankrupt → bankruptcy

dissolute → dissolution

liquidate → liquidation

reorganize → reorganization

corporate → corporation

organize → organization

expire → expiration

remove → removal

distribute → distribution

（二）動詞 → 身分類名詞

manage → manager

share → shareholder

promote → promoter

bond → bondholder

subscribe → subscriber

第八章　證券法

第一節　美國法

一、緒論

There are two settings for buying and selling securities－issuer transactions and trading transactions. Issuer transactions denote the sale of securities by the issuer to investors, namely, the means businesses raise capital. Trading transactions refers to the purchasing and selling of outstanding securities among investors. Investors trade outstanding securities through securities markets, either stock exchanges or "over-the-counter".

買賣證券有二模式：發行人交易與交易所交易。發行人交易指發行人出賣證券予投資人，為企業籌措資金之方法。交易所交易指在投資人間買賣證券。投資人透過證券市場，即證券交易所或櫃檯，從事證券交易。

Transactions that do not take place on a stock exchange occur in the over-the-counter market. Only dealers and brokers registered with the SEC may engage in securities business both on stock exchanges and in over-the-counter markets.

不在證券交易所進行的交易，則在櫃檯市場進行。只有在證管會登記有案之交易商與仲介商，才可在證券交易所與櫃檯市場從事證券業務。

Stock exchanges provide a place, rules, and procedures for buying and selling securities, and the government strictly regulates them. Basically, to have their securities sold and bought on a stock exchange, a company must list its securities on a given exchange. The Securities and Exchange Commission (SEC) must approve the stock exchange's rules before they take effect.

證券交易所提供買賣證券之場所、規則與程序，並受到政府之嚴格規範。基本上公司想在交易所交易之證券，須在一特定交易所掛牌。交易所的規則在生效前，須先經證管會批准。

The securities laws and regulations are aimed to ensure that investors can acquire accurate and necessary information to make investment decisions and to prohibit fraudulent activities in the securities markets.

證券之法律與規章旨在確保投資人投資決定，能收到正確與必要資訊及禁止證券市場詐欺活動。

二、介紹

Securities regulation in U.S. include both federal and state regulation. The Federal Securities Laws consist of a series of statutes. The two main statutes are The Securities Act of 1933 and The Securities Exchange Act of 1934. The '33 Act governs the issuance of securities by companies, and the '34 Act governs the trading of those securities. Each has a lot of regulations promulgated by the Securities and Exchange Commission. Besides, there are also regulations adopted by the National Association of Securities Dealers, Inc. and the various stock exchanges. In addition, every state has its blue sky law.

美國證券法包括聯邦與各州之證券法。聯邦證券法由許多制定法組成，主要有二個制定法：1933年之證券法與1934年之證券交易所法。1933年法規定公司發行證券，1934年法規範證券的交易。此二法又授權由 SEC 制定了許多規章。全國證券自營商協會公司與各證券交易所也制定了一些規章。此外各州證券法則有所謂藍天法。

（一）Securities Act of 1933 1933年之證券法

1. Require investors receive financial and other significant information concerning securities being offered for public sale.
   規定投資人須收到公開買賣之證券之財務與其他重要資訊。

2. Prohibit deceit, misrepresentations, and other fraud in the sale of securities.
   禁止買賣證券有欺騙、不正陳述及其他詐欺行為。

3. Require disclosure of financial information through registration of securities to enable investors to make informed judgments about investing securities.
   要求透過證券之登記，透露財務資訊，使投資人能對投資證券，作知情之判斷。

4. Securities sold in the U.S. must register and disclose information about the company's properties, business, management and the security to be offered for sale.
   在美國出賣的證券必須登記，透露公司之財產、業務、管理及要出賣之證券。

5. Registration statements and prospectuses become public after filing with SEC.
   登記之說明與招股說明書應在呈送證交會後公開。

（二）Securities Exchange Act of 1934 1934年之證券交易法

1. Congress set up the Securities and Exchange Commission (SEC) and empowers SEC with broad authority over the securities industry with power to register, regulate, and oversee brokerage firms, transfer agents, and clearing agencies as well as the nation's securities self regulatory organizations (SROs), such as The Financial Industry Regulatory Authority (FINRA).

國會設立了證券與交易所委員會，被賦予對證券業廣泛的權力，包括登記、規範及監督經紀公司、移轉代理人、票據交換所以及國內證券自律機構（SROs），例如金融業管理局（FINRA）。

2. Exchanges, brokers and dealers, transfer agents, and clearing agencies must register and file disclosure documents regularly with SEC. It prohibits fraudulent activities in connection with the offer, purchase, or sale of securities including fraudulent insider trading and gives SEC disciplinary powers over regulated entities and persons (officers, director, and chief shareholders). SEC requires periodic reporting of information by companies with publicly traded securities. Materials used to solicit shareholders' votes in the election of directors etc. must also file with SEC.

交易所、經紀商、零售商、移轉代理人及票據交換所須向證交會登記並經常呈送透露文件。該法禁止任何有關證券發行與買賣之詐欺活動，包括詐欺內線交易。證交會對被規範之公司及其高層職員、董事及主要股東有懲戒權。該法要求公開交易證券的公司，須向證交會定期呈報各種報告。用來收購選舉董事等之股東表決權的資訊，亦須呈送證交會。

3. The exchanges and the Financial Industry Regulatory Authority (FINRA) are self-regulatory organizations and must create rules for disciplining members for improper conduct and to ensure market integrity and investor protection.

交易所與金融業管理局（FINRA）為自律機構，須訂立規則懲戒會員不當行為與維護市場公正與保護投資人。

三、相關問題

1. Securities Fraud 證券詐欺

Securities fraud include high yield investment fraud, Ponzi and pyramid schemes, broker embezzlement, and advance fee schemes. Besides, insider trading, falsifying information in corporate filings, lying to corporate auditors and manipulating share prices are also securities fraud. They are characterized by the misrepresentation of material information to investors in connection with the sale or purchase of securities and/or the manipulation of financial markets.

證券詐欺包含高收入投資詐欺、老鼠會、經紀人侵占及預收費計畫。此外內線交易、公司呈報假資訊、對公司查帳人說謊、操縱股價等亦然。其特色是有關證券買賣之重要資訊對消費者有不正表述及／或金融市場之操縱。*

* 此係依美國聯邦調查局之見解，範圍頗為廣泛。

2. Insider Trading 內線交易

It means a person trades a security while in possession of material nonpublic information about the company in violation of a duty to withhold the information or refrain from trading. It is illegal because it is unfair to other investors who do not have access to the information. Besides, insider information could potentially make larger profits than a typical investor.

內線交易是當某人交易證券時，擁有該公司重要不公開資訊，而違反不透露資訊或避免交易之義務。此乃違法，因對無資訊之投資人不公平。何況內線資訊可能比平常投資人獲得更多利益。

3. The Elements of Securities Fraud 證券詐欺之要件

The elements of securities fraud require an intentional misrepresentation or omission of material information in connection with the sale or purchase of a security. In addition, plaintiff must also show that they relied on this information, causing losses and ultimately resulting in harm to the plaintiff. The causal relationship between the information or lack-thereof and the resulting harm must be established.

證券詐欺需對某證券買賣之重要資訊有故意不正表述或不提。此外原告須證明其信賴此資訊，且結果受到損失，且證明資訊或欠缺資訊與損失之間有因果關係。

4. Degree of Care 注意義務

In theory, if a particular act did not fall within the scope of the federal securities laws, the actor may still be subject to a fraud claim under the common law. In some states stock brokers may be considered to be fiduciaries to their customers. And they are to conduct with a higher degree of care than the ordinary person.

理論上如某行為非屬聯邦證券法範圍，行為人依普通法仍可能受到詐欺之指控。有些州，證券經紀商可能被認為是客戶之信賴人（受託人），比一般人負較高注意義務。

5. Investment Advisers Act of 1940 1940年投資顧問法

Requires that investment advisers must register with SEC and conform to regulations designed to protect investors.

投資顧問法規定投資顧問須向證交會登記、遵守規則，以保障投資人。

6. Blue Sky Law 藍天法

A blue sky law is a state law regulating the offer and sale of securities, as well as the regulation of broker dealers and stock brokers. It requires registration of securities offerings, and registration of brokers and brokerage firms. Each state has a regulatory agency which administers the law, known as the state Securities Commissioner.

While blue sky laws vary by state, they all aim to protect individuals from fraudulent or overly speculative investments.

各州證券法通稱為藍天法，規範證券之發行與買賣、管理經紀商與交易商。規定發行證券、經紀商與經紀公司都需登記。每州執行此法律之機構稱為州證管會。雖然各州藍天法不同，但都旨在保護投資人免於作詐欺或過度投機性投資。

7. Injunction 禁制令

States allow injunctions to stop businesses from potentially fraudulent activity and give broad investigative power, generally to the attorney general, to investigate fraudulent activity.

各州准許發禁制令，制止廠商潛在的詐欺行為，通常賦予檢察長廣泛的調查權。

（注）本文參考：

1. The Laws That Govern the Securities Industry
   https://www.investor.gov/introduction-investing/investing-basics/role-sec/laws-govern-securities-industry

2. Federal Securities Law, a Securities Lawyer Guide https://www.seclaw.com/federal-securities-law/Share TweetMark J. Astarita

3. Securities law: an overview
   https://www.law.cornell.edu/wex/securities

4. Blue sky law 藍天法
   https://www.law.cornell.edu/wex/blue_sky_law

5. The Guide to Securities Fraud Elements and SEC Rule 10b-5
   https://bnsklaw.com/securities-fraud-sec-rule-10b-5/

6. Securities Fraud Awareness & Prevention Tips
   https://www.fbi.gov/stats-services/publications/securities-fraud

四、詞彙

securities：證券

notes, stocks, bond：股票、債券

short term notes：短期票券

treasury stocks：庫藏股

outstanding securities：已發行尚未償還之證券

voting trust certificates：表決權信託契約

transferable shares：可轉讓股

mineral rights：礦業權

investment contracts：投資契約

home mortgage：房屋抵押

trust indenture：公司債信託契約

bondholder：債券持有人

debentures：公司債

forward contracts：遠期合約

financial derivative：金融衍生品

options on futures：期貨選擇權

futures contract：期貨契約

derivative trading：衍生交易

accounts receivable：應收帳款

raise capital：籌措資金

make informed judgments：作有資訊之判斷

offerings of securities：證券募集

exempting：免除

prospectuses：招股說明

proxy solicitations：徵求委託書

tender offers：投標

nonpublic information：非公開資訊

go into effect：生效

investment advisers：投資顧問

financial statements：財務報告

certified by independent accountants：由獨立會計師簽證

be on the lookout：謹防

insider trading：內線交易

deceit：欺詐

misrepresentations：不正陳述

advance fee schemes：預付費計畫

perpetrators：犯人

high pressure sales tactics：高壓力買賣計畫

unsolicited：不請自來的

solicitor：推銷員

promoter：推銷商

current annual report：當年年報

offering circular：招股傳單

scams：詐騙

manipulating share prices：操作股價

manipulative and deceptive devices and contrivances：操縱與欺詐性之方法與計策

falsifying information in corporate filings：在公司提送之文件作假

lying to corporate auditors：對公司監查人說謊

Ponzi and pyramid schemes：老鼠會

broker embezzlement：經紀人侵占

fraudulent or overly speculative investments：詐欺或過度投機性投資

highly speculative or fraudulent schemes：非常投機性或詐欺策略

promising high investment returns：承諾高投資收益

high yield investment fraud：高收益投資欺罔

comply with：遵守、符合

prospective purchaser：可能買受人

issuer transactions：發行人交易

trading transactions：上市交易

over-the-counter (OTC)：上櫃

physical trading：有形交易

derivatives trading：衍生交易

clearing houses：交易所

Securities and Exchange Commission：證券與交易所委員會

brokerage firms：經紀公司

transfer agents：移轉代理人

clearing agencies：票據交換所

self regulatory organizations：自律機構

New York Stock Exchange：紐約證券交易所

the NASDAQ Stock：納斯達克證券市場

The Financial Industry Regulatory Authority (FINRA)：金融業管理局

Federal Bureau of Investigation：聯邦調查局

state securities regulator：州證券規範機關

a law enforcement agency：執法機關

attorney general：司法部長（檢察長）

stock exchanges or over-the-counter：證券交易所或上櫃

issuer：發行人

disciplinary powers：懲戒權力

periodic reporting：定期報告

publicly traded securities：公開交易證券

merged with：與……合併

common stocks：普通股

interstate commerce：州際通商

subject to certain exemptions：除了若干例外外

exotic investments：外國投資

misinforming investors about：告知錯誤訊息

investment risks：投資風險

oversight of：忽視……

licensed by：由……發執照

additional certifications：其他證照

right of action：訴權（起訴權）

rescission of the transactions：解除交易

breach of fiduciary duty：違反信任義務

regulation：規範、管理

subject to state registration laws：受各州登記法律之規範

per a state's blue skies laws：依一州的藍天法

causes of action：訴因

including but not limited to：包括但不限於

annuity contract：年金契約

insurance policy：保險單

charitable organizations：慈善機構

issued or guaranteed by：由……發行或保證

municipality：市

government entity：政府機構

第二節　我國法

　　Our Securities Law is a special law of corporation law. It was influenced by U.S. law. But U.S. law consists of both statutes and common law, whereas our law is a written law. Our law covers issuance market and trading market, securities issuers and securities investors. Our Securities law has broader scope than U.S. law.

　　我國證券交易法乃公司法之特別法，受美國法影響大，但美國法制定法與判例法並行，我國法乃成文法，仍與美國法差異不少。

我國法內容涵蓋：發行市場及流通市場，有價證券發行人及證券投資人等，規範範圍似較美國法為廣。

Basically it includes the following:

1. Public placement of securities.
2. Publicity of information principle.
3. Corporate governance.
4. Shareholder meetings of public-companies.
5. Regulation of negotiable market, including banning: (1)inside trading; (2)manipulation of market; (3)short term trading.

主要包括下列：

1. 有價證券之招募：含募集（對不特定人）與私募。
2. 資訊公開原則：禁止公開說明書不實與財務不實。
3. 公司治理：含獨立董事、審計委員會、薪酬委員會、委託書與庫藏股。
4. 公開發行公司之股東會。
5. 流通市場管制〔移轉予其他證券投資人（上市與上櫃）〕，包含禁止：(1)內線交易；(2)操縱市場（炒股票）；(3)短線交易。

第三節　習題

選擇題（四選一）

1. The object of Securities Act of 1933 is to prohibit _____.
   (1) deceit & other fraud in the sale of securities
   (2) fraud in the Wall Street
   (3) fraud in the cabinet
   (4) fraud in over-the-counter trade

2. The Securities Act of 1933 requires disclosure of important financial information through _____.

(1) registration of a few securities

(2) registration of securities

(3) registration of brokers and dealers

(4) registration of investment advisers

3. The Securities Act of 1933 designs to make the investors have full information about _____.

(1) the securities he wants to buy

(2) the securities market

(3) New York Stock Exchange

(4) insider trading

4. Pursuant to Securities Exchange Act of 1934, Congress created _____.

(1) New York Stock Exchange

(2) the Securities and Exchange Commission

(3) Trade Representative

(4) Federal Trade Commission

5. Insider trading is illegal when a person trades a security while in possession of material nonpublic information in violation of a duty to _____.

(1) invest

(2) trade

(3) keep secret

(4) withhold the information or refrain from trading

6. Ponzi and pyramid schemes are an example of _____.

(1) investment

(2) trade

(3) fraud

(4) business strategy

7. Blue Sky laws was enacted in _____.

(1) some states

(2) many states

(3) some territories

(4) all states

8. Prospectuses means _____.

(1) 股務代理

(2) 招股說明書

(3) 財務報告

(4) 會計準則

9. Over the Counter is a decentralized market where financial securities are sold and bought by _____ directly through computer networks and phone.

(1) brokers and brokers

(2) brokers and dealers

(3) investors and dealers

(4) investors and brokers

10. Stock exchange is a centralized market where buying and selling of stocks occurs between _____ in a transparent and systematic way.

(1) brokers and dealers

(2) buyers and sellers

(3) merchants

(4) investors

11. A derivative denotes a financial contract that derive their value from an underlying asset. The value of the underlying asset keeps on changing depending on the market conditions. The buyer agrees to buy the asset on a specific date at a specific price. It is often used for _____, such as oil, gasoline, or gold.

(1) U.S. dollar

(2) options

(3) swaps

(4) commodities

12. A _____ is a contract between two parties to trade certain commodity asset of specific quantity at a predetermined price at a specified date in future.

(1) stock

(2) futures contract

(3) option contract

(4) swap contract

13. The 1934 Act grants the SEC the authority to register, regulate, and oversee _____ and clearing agencies as well as the country's securities self -regulatory organizations (SROs).

(1) visitors

(2) brokerage firms, transfer agents,

(3) investors

(4) board directors

14. Securities fraud, according to the Federal Bureau of Investigation, includes a broad range of activities, including but not limited to high yield investment fraud, _____, broker embezzlement, and advance fee schemes.

(1) brokers fraud

(2) eaminers' corruption

(3) Ponzi and pyramid schemes

(4) dealer fraud

15. Securities fraud is characterized by the misrepresentation of material information to investors in connection with the sale or purchase of securities and/or the _____.

    (1) manipulation

    (2) pyramid

    (3) Ponzi

    (4) manipulation of financial markets

16. The SEC often serves as plaintiff in securities fraud lawsuits. In addition, private plaintiffs may sue if they have _____, i.e., they were directly harmed by the securities fraud. Private parties that were not directly targeted by the securities fraud may seek recourse by bringing the issue to the attention of the SEC.

    (1) cause of action

    (2) standing

    (3) status

    (4) position

17. Securities fraud is a serious white-collar crime and can lead to both criminal and civil penalties. The SEC often serves as plaintiff in filing securities fraud lawsuits. Private plaintiffs also have standing to do so if they were the defrauded investor. Investors that were not directly targeted by securities fraud may notify _____ to investigate and prosecute the alleged violation.

    (1) attorney general

    (2) FTC

    (3) the SEC

    (4) court

18. A blue sky law is a _____ law regulating the offer and sale of securities, as well as the regulation of broker dealers and stock brokers. The laws require registration of securities offerings, and registration of brokers and brokerage firms.

    (1) criminal

    (2) state

    (3) national

    (4) federal

19. A blue sky law is a state law regulating the offer and sale of _____, as well as the regulation of broker dealers and stock brokers. The laws require registration of _____ offerings, and registration of brokers and brokerage firms.

    (1) gold

    (2) commodity

    (3) bonds

    (4) securities

20. The Securities Exchange Act of 1934 grants the _____ with wide supervision power over the securities industry.

    (1) attorney general

    (2) FTC

    (3) SEC

    (4) court

21. Materials used to _____ shareholders' votes in the election of directors etc. must disclose all important facts concerning the issues and filed with the commission in advance.

    (1) sell

    (2) solicit

    (3) buy

    (4) trade

22. The common law notions of contract and _____ also find their way into the securities laws, for each purchase and sale of a security is a contract, and each transaction between market participants, can involve issues of _____ law.

    (1) corporation

    (2) criminal

    (3) tort

    (4) negligence

23. Insider trading means buying or selling a public company's stock or other securities based on material, _____ about the company. It is illegal because it is unfair to other investors who have no access to such information. Moreover, people with insider information can possibly earn larger profits than other investors.

    (1) fiducial information

    (2) information

    (3) nonpublic information

    (4) confidential information

▲選擇題解答

1. (1)	2. (2)	3. (1)	4. (2)	5. (4)	6. (3)	7. (4)	8. (2)	9. (2)
10. (2)	11. (4)	12. (2)	13. (2)	14. (3)	15. (4)	16. (2)	17. (3)	18. (2)
19. (4)	20. (3)	21. (2)	22. (4)	23. (3)				

第四節　詞彙整理

一、同義詞或類似詞

fraud－scams－deceit

conceal－false information－
　misrepresentations

empower－authorize

register, registration－regulate－
　oversee－control

incomplete－inaccurate

proxy－power of attorney

act－law

regulation－guideline－decree

market－exchange

stock－bond

certificate－security－futures

sale－trade

investor－dealer－broker

paragraph－article

二、詞性轉換

（一）動詞 → 名詞

disclose → disclosure

solicit → solicitation

explain → explanation

enforce → enforcement

（二）名詞 → 形容詞

discipline → disciplinary

regulation → regulatory

prospect → prospective

transfer → transferable

第九章　民事訴訟法

第一節　美國法

The American civil procedure law is extremely complex and the federal system make it even more so. Yet their reference materials are highly scarce in Taiwan.

美國民事訴訟法異常繁複，聯邦制度使其複雜性加深，然國內相關資料奇缺。

一、特色

1. Attorneys lead the proceeding, the judges' roles are rather negative.
   律師主導訴訟進行，法官角色消極。
2. Jury system are adopted.
   有陪審制度。
3. Court fees are cheap. Appeal fee s are uniform regardless the amount of the controversy.
   法院裁判費低廉，上訴審訴訟費用一致，而與訴訟標的之價額多少無關。
4. Contingent fee and legal aid help poor plaintiffs have access to the court.
   律師費准許成功報酬（contingent fee）制度*，加上法律扶助制度致財力不足之人原則上亦可提起訴訟。

   ＊ 所謂成功報酬乃當事人起訴時不給律師酬金，俟和解或勝訴時，再分所得，例如將40%付給律師。

5. Controversy of public law are also governed by civil procedure and decided by ordinary civil courts.

公法爭議亦適用民事訴訟法規定，且由普通法院管轄。行政與司法案件歸普通法院管轄。

6. Concentrated trials are adopted by courts.

集中審理（因採陪審制度，故須集中審理，連續不中斷）。

7. Precedent theories and test case practice may help decrease litigation.

有先例理論或試驗案件（test case）制度*，可減少訟源。

　*　試驗案件是一種法律訴訟，目的在確立一種先例。例如，提出訴訟目的在觀察法院是否對一定情況，適用某種法律或先例，以便在事後在類似情況提出類似訴訟。有時律師在試驗案件判決前暫緩起訴。政府機關有時也提起試驗案件，以確認或擴大其權限。

8. Both parties should develop evidence by discovery. Such mechanism are well developed including pretrial discovery and interrogatories, etc.

當事人須開發證據，各種證據開示機制發達，便於當事人（尤其對原告有利）。舉證開示方法頗多，包括律師可在審理庭前訊問證人取得證言，並可以書面詢問單（interrogatories）要求對造答覆等。

9. Class actions lawsuits help many victims of small claims to get compensation.

有集體訴訟制度，使訴訟標的小額之多數被害人便於獲得救濟。

10. Injunctions may be used as a kind of final remedy in addition to temporary remedy and may exert bigger roles.

禁制令（injunction）*除定暫時狀態外，尚可作為終局救濟，尤其不限於禁止被告為一定行為，亦可命其為一定行為，而發揮莫大作用。

*　禁制令與我民訴法假處分有點類似，但範圍與效用更廣。

11. Motions are particularly used by both parties.
    盛行聲請法院為一定行為（motions）*，有利案件之速結。
    * motion有人譯為動議，實則不對。

12. Pretrial conference helps accelerate solution of the controversy.
    採用預審會議制度，加速爭議之解決。

13. Both parties may serve as witness.
    當事人亦可作證，此點亦與我國法不同。

14. Conversation between certain people may not be compelled to disclose in court. This is called a privilege. Such as attorney client privilege, spousal privilege.
    若干關係之人之間談話，不可強制在法庭透露，稱為特權（privilege）。

15. Expert witnesses are provided by the parties and paid by them.
    鑑定人由當事人自行物色與付費。

16. Contempt of court may be used to find the property of the debtor in a supplementary proceeding.
    有蔑視法庭制度，有利於事實之發現或所命義務之履行，且便於發現債務人財產與強制執行〔稱為補助程序（supplementary proceedings）〕。

17. Around 85% of civil cases are settled before trial after the pretrial conference.
    約85%的民事案件於預審會議後，即在審理前解決。且大多數訴訟於審理前由和解而解決。

18. As a rule one level of trial will end the litigation. In certain states the winning judgment may automatically be imposed for the creditor a legal pledge upon the debtor's real property.
    原則一審終結。一審勝訴判決有些州自動對債務人之財產取得法定留置權，即可執行。

19. American courts in rendering the judgments often consider the possible impact of such decision on the society.
美國法院判決往往會注意結果對社會可能發生之影響。

20. Civil appeal as a rule does not stop execution of the judgment. But the appellant may pay a bond to stop the execution.
民事上訴，原則不停止判決之執行，但上訴人可繳納上訴擔保金，阻止其執行。

21. Appeals are not retrial of the case. The appellate court usually does not consider new witnesses or new evidence.
上訴不是案件的再審或重新審理，上訴法院通常不考慮新證人或新證據。

22. Dissenting opinions may also be presented in judgment of an appellate court.
上級法院法官在判決上可提不同意。

23. Amicus Curiae are recognized in an appellate court.
美國有法庭之友書狀（Amicus Curiae）制度*。
   * 對案件結果有利害關係之人或機構，可經上級法院准許，以書狀提意見，供該法院辦案之參酌，與審判獨立無涉。

24. Execution procedure are usually simplified and swift.
強制執行手續簡便。

25. Civil procedural law (rules) are enacted by the Supreme Court.
民事訴訟法（稱為規則）係由最高法院制定。

26. People often resort to litigation so that litigations are over-flooded.
人民好訟成風，訴訟氾濫。

27. U.S. courts recognize forum non conveniens theory.
有法庭不方便制度（forum non conveniens），如後所述。

28. The plaintiffs tend to find the most favorable court (jurisdiction) for them. This is where the term "forum shopping" comes from.
原告有挑選法庭（forum shopping）現象*。
   * 指當事人選擇案件由可能判決之法院管轄的現象。

二、介紹

（一）Overview 概述

1. While most civil cases are handled in state courts, federal courts handle federal question cases and exclusive jurisdiction cases (admiralty and maritime law, bankruptcy, patent, trademark and copyright law) and diversity citizenship cases.

美國民事訴訟採聯邦與各州二元制（法院與法律均有兩套），多數訴訟案件係由州法院受理。聯邦法院只處理聯邦問題案件*與專屬管轄案件（包括海商、保險、破產、專利、商標與著作權）及不同州籍公民間案件。

   ＊ 聯邦問題案件係指違反聯邦憲法、聯邦法律或當事人一方為美國之條約的案件。

2. In a case both the state and federal courts have concurrent jurisdiction, e.g., "diversity jurisdiction" in a state court, cases involving people who live in different states and are in dispute over property valued at US$75,000 or more, the defendant may have the case transferred, or "removed" to federal court.

案件在聯邦與州法院有競合管轄權，例如涉及外州公民，且標的價額超過美金7萬5,000元時，被告可要求州法院將案件移歸（transfer）聯邦法院管轄。

3. Unlike civil law countries, the law governing civil procedure is not enacted by the Congress, The Federal Rules of Civil Procedure was enacted by the Supreme Court governing civil proceedings in the United States district courts. Every state has its own civil procedure rules basically similar to the federal rules.

美國民事訴訟法不似大陸法系國家，是由立法機關訂定，聯邦係由最高法院制定「聯邦民事訴訟規則」（The Federal Rules of Civil Procedure），規範聯邦地方法院民事訴訟，各州亦有自己的訴訟規則，基本上與聯邦規則近似。

4. The court have three levels: trial courts (District Courts), then intermediate Appeals Courts (Courts of Appeal), finally the Supreme Court. Cases in federal court may be appealed from a trial court (district court)to the federal Court of Appeals for that particular circuit, and then by writ of certiorari to the United States Supreme Court.

聯邦法院有三級，地方法院、上訴法院、最高法院。聯邦法院案件可自地院上訴至該區之上訴法院，再經由移審令到最高法院。

5. All courts, both federal and state, must follow any precedent set by the Supreme Court and should look to precedent when making their decisions.

所有聯邦與州法院須遵守最高法院所訂先例（precedent）*，於下判決時亦然。

* 稱為遵循先例原則（stare decisis）。

（二）Civil Litigation 民事訴訟

1. Complaint 起訴狀

To begin a civil lawsuit, the plaintiff files a complaint with the court and "serves" a copy on the defendant describing the plaintiff's damages or injury, explains how the defendant caused the harm, and asks the court to order relief.

法院之民事訴訟因原告*提訴狀予法院，送達**一份予被告***，敘明原告之損害，解釋被告引起損害之經過，並請求法院判令救濟而開始。

*原告須有當事人適格（standing to sue），即對爭訟結果有利害關係。惟其解釋較我國為寬。

**送達須以合理方法，俾被告有機會出庭應訊，通常由專人送達。

***被告對起訴狀須呈送（answer）答辯狀予法院。

A plaintiff may ask the court for damages, or order the defendant to stop the conduct. It may also render a declaration of the legal rights of the plaintiff. The aggrieved party may apply a court for specific performance for both action or omission, but only granted in special occasion, such as delivery of a specific piece of land.

原告可請求法院命被告損害賠償，或命被告停止其行為，亦可宣告原告之法律上權利。被害人亦可申請法院對被告之作為或不作為發禁制令（injunction），不過法院只在例外情況才會准許（例如交付特定土地）。*

*原告提起訴訟時應支付法定之遞狀費（filing fee）。無力繳費之原告可依據訴訟救助（forma pauperis）呈請免繳。又訴訟文書之送達與我國不同，並不盡採郵寄方式。

2. Jurisdiction 管轄權

(1) Personal Jurisdiction and Subject Matter Jurisdiction 人的管轄權與事物管轄權

A court must have jurisdiction to enter a judgment. Jurisdiction may be divided into: personal jurisdiction and subject matter jurisdiction. Personal jurisdiction is a court has power over the defendant, based on minimum contacts with the forum. Subject-matter jurisdiction is a court has power to hear the specific kind of claim. Personal jurisdiction may be waived but not subject-matter jurisdiction.

法院須有管轄權始能下判決。管轄權可分為人的管轄權與事物管轄權。前者指法院基於被告與法庭地有最低接觸而來。事物管轄權係指對事件標的有權管轄。前者可放棄，後者則不可。

(2) Jurisdiction in Personam vs. Jurisdiction in Rem 對人管轄權與對物管轄權

Jurisdiction can also divided into jurisdiction in Personam and jurisdiction in Rem. Jurisdiction in personam means that an action must be filed in the court where the defendant presents and a judgment can be enforced there. If the lawsuit is to determine title to property (in rem) the action must be filed in the court where the property locates and can only be enforced there.

管轄權又分為對人管轄權與對物管轄權。對人管轄權指應在被告所在地起訴與執行訴訟，反之，對物管轄權指有關財產權利之訴訟，須向財產所在地起訴與執行。

(3) Forum Non-conveniens 不方便法庭地原則

Forum non-conveniens ("inconvenient forum" doctrine) allows a court to dismiss or transfer a case, even one filed properly in a permissible venue, if an alternative forum is available and would be more convenient to the parties and witnesses. E.g., transfer the case to the court of the place where the event causing the dispute occurred or to the court where most witnesses reside.

美國有所謂不方便法庭地原則，即使法庭地適當，且法院對該案與當事人有管轄權，如有更方便被告與證人之法庭地時，法院可駁回或移轉原告之訴。例如將案件移交發生訴訟所依據事故以及所有證人居住的法院，以期公平。

3. Parties 當事人

The federal rules concerning parties, including joinder, cross-claim, impleader, etc., are almost unknown in our civil procedure law and terribly complicated beyond comprehension of lawyers of civil law countries. Thus omitted here.

美國聯邦規則有關當事人之規定，包括請求權合併、交互訴訟、第三人被告等制度，多為我國民訴法所無，且極為繁雜，非大陸法系法律人所易理解，且超出司法應考範圍，故此處從略*。

*讀者如欲知其詳，可參照楊崇森，遨遊美國法，第三冊第三章，美國民事訴訟制度之特色與對我國之啟示，頁47以下。

在美國法：

(1) 請求權等合併（joinder）之規定頗爲寬鬆，便於當事人起訴 與符合訴訟經濟。

(2) 有第三人訴訟或第三人被告（impleader）制度。

(3) 承認交互訴訟（cross claim）制度，使被告可於同一訴訟對共 同被告追究責任。

4. Class Action 集體訴訟

In order to prevent risk of inconsistent results, one or more representatives of a group of people with similar claims (e.g., mass tort cases involving personal injuries, such as airplane accident) can file suit on behalf the entire group.

所謂集體訴訟係指有共同問題（有類似請求）之一群人，爲防 止各別判決不一致，可由一人或數人代表此群人起訴*多見於被害 人眾多之損害賠償訴訟（如飛機事故）。

*出名當事人須能充分代表未參加之成員之利益，原則上所有成員 受判決之拘束。

5. Trial Date 審理日期

The judge will issue a scheduling order laying out a timeline for important dates and deadlines, including the trial date.

法官會發下時間表，定出重要日期與截止日，包括審理日 期。*

*民事案件在舉行審理庭本身前，在法官前也有許多所謂調查庭 （hearing），目的在於給雙方表示意見之機會。包括定調查庭之 日期、對聲請之准駁、對證據調查之准駁、對證據之准駁等。

6. Case Preparation and Pretrial Conference 案件準備與預審會議

Civil litigation in U.S. adopts adversary system as well as concentrated and continuous trial. The attorneys of both sides play important role. Both parties may use "discovery" to assemble evidence and prepare to call witnesses. They have the following tools to obtain information:

　　美國民事訴訟採當事人進行主義（對立主義）與集中連續審理主義（審理一次完成），雙方之律師扮演重要角色，雙方可用「證據開示」＊（相當於我們的證據調查）蒐集證據與傳喚證人。開示有下列方法：

＊由雙方律師發見或提出證據，爲了防止審理時一方提出證據使對方措手不及，並鼓勵雙方和解，審理前證據開示（discovery）極爲重要。

(1) Depositions 法庭外取證

A party can require a witness to answer questions about the case before the trial. The witness answers questions from the lawyer under oath, in the presence of a court reporter, who produces a transcript (a word-for-word account).

　　一造當事人可於審理前要求證人對該案答覆律師所提問題，證人於宣誓後在法院速記員（作逐句筆錄）前，答覆問題。＊

＊法庭外採取證人證言（目的在保全證據等）的方法，也用法庭上問答之形式，須通知所有當事人到場，並由其律師交互詰問證人。

(2) Interrogatories 問題單

A party can require other parties (but not witnesses) to answer 25 questions in writing. The other party should answer under oath. It is very helpful to acquire evidence held by the other party.

　　一造當事人可寄發問題單（問題限25個以內）給對造（證人則不可），對造須宣誓後用書面答覆。此方法對取得對造占有下之證據，非常有用。

(3) Document Requests 要求交付文件等證物

A party can seek documents and other real objects from parties and non parties. If any trade secrets is involved, the other party may request the court to issue a protective order as a deterrence.

一造律師可要求檢閱對造及第三人手中的文件與其他物品。若請求涉及營業秘密時，則被請求人可申請法官發保護令，以資抑制。

(4) Motions for Physical or Mental Examination 檢查身心

If a person whose bodily condition is in issue, a party may apply the court to demand him to receive physical or mental examination by a medical doctor. The disadvantage of discovery is too costly and may impose burden on third parties.

如爭議涉及一造之身心狀態時，當事人可聲請法院命該人接受醫生為其作身體或心理檢查。惟開示制度之缺點是花費太多，且可能使第三人被課以義務，造成不便。

(5) Pretrial Conference 預審會議*

If necessary, a meeting of the judge and lawyers is to be held in order to plan the trial, to discuss which matters should be presented to the jury, to review proposed evidence and witnesses, and to set a trial schedule. Some pretrials are held in court in front of the judge, some are more like meetings between the two sides. There is no limit on the number of pretrial conferences. Most cases are settled before this stage; perhaps 85 percent of all civil cases end before trial.

必要時由法官與雙方律師開會（pretrial conference）籌劃審理事項，討論何種事務提交陪審，檢討證據與證人，並定下審理日程。有些預審會議在法官前進行，有些較類似兩造之間會商，其次數不限。大多數民事案件（約85%）於此階段，即審理前解決。

*關於預審會議之詳細情形，可參照楊崇森，遨遊美國法，第三冊第八章，美國預審制度，頁273以下（尤其所附預審程序舉隅，更可了解美國預審之實際運作情形）。

7. Rules of Evidence 證據法則

The basic prerequisites of admissibility are relevance, materiality, and competence. In general, if evidence is shown to be relevant, material, and competent, and is not barred by an exclusionary rule, it is admissible. The exclusionary rule is based on constitutional law, that prevents evidence collected or analyzed in violation of the defendant's constitutional rights from being used in a court.

證據採用與否，要看其有無具備相關性、重要性及適格性。通常如某證據與案情相關、重要與適格，且不在排除原則之列，則可接納爲證據。*排除證據之原則乃基於憲法防止法院違反被告憲法上權利蒐集分析證據而來。

*美國證據法極爲複雜。

Exclusion of Evidence 排除之證據

(A) hearsay evidence 傳聞證據。

(B) privilege 特權：

Protects communications within certain relationships from compelled disclosure in a court proceeding. Including:

(a) attorney-client communications.

(b) lawyer's work-product (e.g., witness interviews).

(c) physician-patient communications.

(d) privilege against self-incrimination.

保護具有若干關係之人之間談話，不可強制在法庭透露*，包含：

(a) 律師與當事人間之談話。

(b) 律師之工作成果（例如訪問證人）。

(c) 醫師與病人間之談話。

(d) 避免自證有罪。

*美國法在若干情形，證人不必向法院透露談話內容，稱爲特權（privilege），因認爲維護私密，比在案件審判取得資訊更爲重

要。此特權係基於相關關係之性質而來，因如不予保護，則當事人不與其律師締結機密之關係、病人可能不敢看醫生、信徒可能不欲見傳道人、夫妻可能不推心置腹信賴對方。

8. Motion 聲請*

Motion are made frequently by both parties. A motion is a request by a party that the court take specified action. Motions can address almost any substantive or procedural aspect of the case, including pretrial, during the trial and post-trial. E.g., pretrial motions may address to the court's competence and proper venue, the scope of the litigation, pretrial procedure itself or the merits of the case.

當事人之律師常多利用聲請（motion）。所謂聲請是指當事人一方要求法院為特定行為。聲請幾乎可針對案件的任何實體或程序問題提出，且包括預審、審理中及判決後。例如預審的聲請可對法院管轄權及正當審判地、訴訟之範圍、預審程序本身或案件之勝負提出。

*motion 為英美民刑訴訟制度之特殊機制，我國民事訴訟法並無與其類似之機制，無適當中文表達。

9. Settling Differences 解決爭議

To avoid the expense and delay of a trial, judges encourage the parties to use mediation, arbitration to solve dispute. Absent a settlement, the court will schedule a trial. If the parties waive their right to a jury, then a judge will hear the case.

為了避免審理之費用與延擱，法官鼓勵雙方用調解、仲裁解決爭議。如不能和解，則由法院定期審理*。如雙方放棄陪審審判**，則由法官自己聽訟。

*大多數訴訟於審理前由和解而解決。

**陪審團原則不得少於6人，決議原則須全員一致。否則構成失審（mistrial），必須從選任陪審員起，重新進行審理（retrial）。

10. Trial Process 審理程序

The judge plays a negative role in trial.

開庭時法官角色消極。

(1) Witness: The opposing attorney may object if a question of the opposing attorney invites the witness to say something prejudicial, or irrelevant to the case. The judge either overrules or sustains (allows) the objection. If the objection is sustained, the witness needs not to answer the question, and the attorney must move on to his next question. The court reporter records the objections so that a court of appeals can review the arguments later if necessary.

如對方律師邀證人說一些偏見或與案件無關的話，對造律師可提出異議。法官可對異議予以駁回或維持（准許）。如異議被法官維持，則證人不必答覆問題，該律師應問下一個問題。法院速記員應將異議記錄下來，俾上級法院事後必要時可審查該辯論。

(2) Expert witness: Expert witness is provided and paid by the party. His credibility is subject to challenge.

鑑定人由當事人提供並負擔費用，其可信度（含專業程度等）可受挑戰。[*]

[*] 鑑定人在英美法稱為專家證人（expert witness），乃一種特殊證人，與我國法不同。

(3) The party may also serve as witness.

當事人亦可作證。[*]

[*] 此點亦與我國法不同。

(4) Exhibits (documents and other tangible evidences) must be authenticated and admitted during the trial. Before trial, the parties may try to agree on which documents or devices will be brought in trial for judge or jury inspection.

證據（書證與其他有形證據）應在審理庭確認與列為證據（加上號數）。當事人間可能在審理前先就哪些物證要提出成立協議（stipulation）。

11. Summary Judgment 簡易判決

Either party can file a "motion for summary judgment" by showing no material dispute between the parties and he is entitled to win as a matter of law.

原告或被告皆可提簡易判決之聲請,證明當事人間並無重要爭執,且聲請人法律上有權勝訴。*

*此時法官可不開庭審理而直接對全部或部分案件下實體判決。如此可加速訴訟進程,節省訴訟成本,是英美法有特色的制度。

12. Closing 結束

After evidence is presented, each side makes a closing argument (or charge), which is the lawyer's final opportunity to tell the judge and/or jury why they should win the case. They explain how the evidence supports their theory of the case, and by clarifying any issues that the jury must resolve in a verdict. They often employ creative strategies and techniques to do so. Then in a jury trial, the judge will explain the pertinent law and the decisions the jury needs to make. The jury should determine whether the defendant is liable for the plaintiff's claim and determine the amount of damages to pay. In a non-jury case, the judge will decide these issues. In a civil case, the plaintiff must convince the jury by a "preponderance of the evidence" (more likely than not).

雙方提出證據完畢後,由兩造作結束辯論。這是律師告知法官及/或陪審團他應該勝訴之理由的最後機會。他們常用有創意的策略與技巧,解釋證據如何支持他對該案的看法,澄清陪審團在裁決*應解決之爭點。然後在陪審審判,法官向陪審團(口頭)**解釋有關法律及陪審團須決定被告應否負責及要付之賠償額(稱為 jury instructions)。在無陪審案件,則由法官決定這些爭點。在民事案件,原告須以較強(即較為可能)之證據***說服陪審團,被告應該負責。

＊裁決（verdict）分爲概括裁決（general verdict）與特定裁決（special verdict）兩種，前者陪審團只須提出答案，後者須附上理由。

＊＊近年爲使陪審員明白指示內容，有些法院會給一份書面予陪審團。

＊＊＊如以百分比計算，則刑事案件有罪證據需95%，民事案件勝訴需51%。參照 Burnham, Introduction to the Law and Legal System of the United States (Thomson/West, 2002) p.105.

13. Winning Judgment of the Trial Court May Be Enforced 一審判決可執行

The wining plaintiff may record his judgment lien on the defendant's real property and execute the judgment.

An appeal doesn't ordinarily prevent the enforcement of the trial court's judgment. But the appealing party can file an appeal bond to prevent it.

當原告一審勝訴後，可對被告之財產登錄裁判留置權，加以執行＊。民事案件的上訴＊＊，通常不妨礙審判法院判決之執行，但上訴人可繳納上訴擔保金（file an appeal or supersedeas bond），阻止執行，直到上訴結束。

＊裁判留置權係美國一種法定留置權，在大多數州須向郡書記提出判決，加以登錄，有些州判決會自動附加在被告不動產上。此點與我國判決須確定後方可強制執行，大異其趣。

＊＊美國訴訟費用與上訴費用基本上一律，不問標的價額大小（故窮人較能親近法院），但上訴須檢附印刷多份訴訟紀錄等，所費不貲，往往限制了想上訴之人的數目△。

△Karlen, Civil Litigation in Turkey, (Ankara, 1957).

14. Appeal Procedure 上訴程序

Either party may make appeal in a civil case. There must be a legal basis for the appeal—an alleged material error in the trial procedure or errors in the judge's interpretation of the law. An appeal is not a retrial or a new trial of the case. The appeals courts do not usually consider new witnesses or new evidence.

民事案件雙方均可上訴。上訴須有法律基礎——審理程序有重要錯誤或法官對法律之解釋有誤。上訴不是案件的再審或重新審理，上訴法院通常不考慮新證人或新證據。

The appellant must file a brief and the appellee file an answering brief. Sometimes, appeals courts make decision on the basis of the written briefs. Sometimes, they set for oral argument and ask questions.

上訴人須提上訴案件摘要，被上訴人提答辯理由狀。有時上訴法院只根據書面的案件摘要下判決，有時定下言詞辯論及提出問題。

The appellate court determines whether errors occurred in applying the law at the lower court. It will reverse for admitting improper evidence. The judgment will be drafted by one judge. Judges disagreeing with the majority opinion may file a dissenting opinion. Those disagree with their reasoning may file a concurring opinion.

上級法院審定下級審適用法律有無錯誤，如採用不當證據則加以廢棄。判決由一名法官撰寫。不同意的法官可撰寫不同意見書（dissenting opinion），同意多數意見，但不同意其理由的法官可提出協同意見書（concurring opinion）。

If the appeals court affirms the lower court's judgment, the case ends, unless the losing party appeals to a higher court. The lower court decision also stands if the appeals court simply dismisses the appeal.

如判決確認原判決，則案件結束，除非敗訴一方再上訴。如上訴法院只駁回上訴，則原判決也被維持。

If the judgment is reversed, the appellate court will send the case back to a lower court (remand it) and order it:

(1) hold a new trial.

(2) modify or correct the judgment.

(3) reconsider the facts, take additional evidence, or consider the case in light of a recent decision by the appellate court.

如判決廢棄，通常上訴法院將案件發回（remand）下級法院，並命該法院：

(1) 重新審理。

(2) 修正原判決。

(3) 重新斟酌事實、採更多證據，或參考上訴法院之新近判決處理。

（注）本文參考

1. Civil Cases
   https://www.uscourts.gov/about-federal-courts/types-cases/civil-cases

2. Hazard & Taruffo, American Civil Procedure (Yale University Press, 1993).

3. 楊崇森，遨遊美國法，第三冊第三章，美國民事訴訟法之特色與對我國之啟示，頁47以下。

4. ABA, Appeals, How Court Works
   https://www.americanbar.org/groups/public_education/resources/law_related_education_network/how_courts_work/appeals/

5. Coughlin, Your Introduction to Law (Harper & Row, 1979).

三、詞彙

The Federal Rules of Civil Procedure：聯邦民事訴訟規則

complaint：訴狀

filing fee：遞狀費

forma pauperis：訴訟救助

process：訴訟文件、訴訟書狀

serves：送達

trial court：審判法院

jurisdiction：管轄權，有時指州

action in rem：屬物之訴訟

action in personam：屬人之訴訟

parties：當事人

standing：起訴之資格

counter claim：反訴

opposing attorney：對造

litigant：訴訟當事人

file an action：提起訴訟

domicile：住所

subject matter：標的

forum shopping：挑選對原告可能有利之法庭地（法院）

pending action：訴訟繫屬中

response：回答

summons：傳票

versus：控告

plaintiff or claimant：原告或聲請人

opposing attorney：對造

brief：一造當事人向法院所提表達案件之事實與適用法律之書狀

claim：聲稱、請求權

allegation：主張

answer：答辯

denial：否認

trial lawyer：出庭律師

clerk：書記官

court reporter：速記員

transcript：訴訟紀錄

impleader：第三人參加訴訟

joinder of claims：訴之合併

derivative actions：傳來訴訟

class action：集體訴訟

subpoenas.：傳票

discovery：證據開示

deposition：法庭外採取證言〔指證人在公開法庭外，在宣誓後回答律師口頭詢問（oral examination），並作成筆錄之證詞〕。多爲蒐集證據之用，也可用在審理

protective order：保護令

interrogatories：問題單

physical & mental examinations：身心檢查

obtain document production：取得文件

depositions of non-parties：非當事人之證據開示

pre-trial discovery stage：審理前開示階段

stipulations：協議

exhibit：在審理或開庭作爲證據之文件或他物

pre-trial conference：預審會議

motion：聲請

specified action：特定行爲

trial process (trial proceedings)：審理程序

incompetent：無行爲能力人

hearing date：庭訊日

default judgment：缺席判決

prima facie case：有足夠證據可以成案之案件

summary judgment：簡易判決

witness：證人

expert witness：鑑定人

proof：證據

testimony：證言

evidence：證明

jury system：陪審制

jury trial：陪審審判

voir dire examination：挑選陪審員之詰問

jurors：陪審員

jury：陪審團

direct examination：直接詰問

cross examination：交互詰問

redirect examination：再直接詰問

recross examination：再交互詰問

dismiss (v.) / dismissal (n.)：駁回

overrules or sustains：駁回或維持

objections：異議

resolved：解決

burden of proof：舉證責任

admissible：可採

perpetuate testimony：保存證據

pending action：繫屬於訴訟中

on the merits：實體上

notice：通知

constitutionality：合憲性

closing argument：終結辯論

prevailing party：贏的一方

preponderance of the evidence：證據較強

merits of the case：案件之輸贏

third-party plaintiff & defendant：第三人原告與被告

declaratory judgment：宣告式判決、確認判決

subpoena：傳喚證人

summary judgment：簡易判決

special & general verdict：特定與概括裁決

verdict：裁決

judgment：判決

executed：執行

file an appeal or supersedeas bond：提供上訴擔保金

due process：正當法律程序

consent judgment：認諾判決

provisional remedies：臨時性保全措施

directed verdict / judgment as a matter of law：指案件的證據非常有說服力，或證據未能成立所謂表面案件（establish a prima facie case），直接依法官的命令對案件作出裁判

espondent：被上訴人

motion for a new trial：申請重審

res judicata：既判力

appeal：上訴

appelate court：上訴法院

intermediate appellate court：中間上訴法院

en banc：全院（審理）

ex parte：單方

ex parte proceeding：單方程序

finding：認定

deliberation：評議

harmless error：無害之錯誤

exclusionary rule：禁止審理時使用不法取得之證據之原則

mandamus：法院命某官員為一定行為之令狀

jury commissioner：法院主管陪審之官員

summation：結論

order：除了終局判決以外，任何傳統形式之司法決定（traditional form of for any judicial determination, short of a final judgment disposing of the entire case）

dissenting opinion：不同意見

concurring opinion：協同意見

stands：維持

remand：發回

in light of：參考

reverse：廢棄

reversible error：足使下級審判決廢棄之錯誤

rebuttal：反駁

reasonable person：與我國法上善良管理人相當

third party claim：第三人請求

injunction：禁制令

specific performance：特定履行

taking of testimony：採取證言

open court：公開法庭

enforecement：執行

declaratory judgment：宣言判決

certiorari：最高法院向下級審案件調取令

supplementary proceedings：補充程序、輔助程序*

*即在民事判決發出執行令後，債權人可用此程序申請法院傳債務人到庭答覆財產所在，如債務人違反該裁定，可能以藐視法庭加以羈押。

第二節　我國法

1. Taiwan does not adopt concentrated trial system.
   我國法不採集中審理主義。
2. The judge leads the proceeding. The attorneys' roles are not as important as their counterparts in the U.S..
   由法官而非律師控制訴訟之進行，律師角色重要性不如美國。

3. Taiwan does not have discovery of evidence system as the U.S., therefore the evidence may possibly be incomplete.

並無美國法之證據開示制度，證據可能漏了不少或不夠翔實。

4. The expert witness is appointed by the court.

鑑定人由法院指定。

5. The parties cannot serve as witness.

當事人不可作證。

6. We adopt free evaluation of evidence principle as the other civil law countries.

證據之證明力採自由心證主義，排除證據遠比美國少。

7. The attorneys are not deemed as officers of the court.

律師不是法院職員。

8. There is no jury system.

不採陪審制度。

9. Court system in Taiwan is not as complex as the U.S.

全國法院一元，不似美國有聯邦與州二套法院系統。

10. There is no contempt of court.

無蔑視法庭制度。

11. The parties tend to appeal their case all the way to the Supreme Court and try to exhaust the legal redress. The court fees are high since they are charged basing on the disputed monetary value of the subject matter. The attorney fees are not as high as in the U.S.

當事人常一直上訴到底，訴訟費用按標的價額計算，費用較高，與美國一致的費用不同。律師費則不如美國高。

12. The process of execution is very complex.

強制執行手續繁複。

13. The law has no restriction for execution of specific subject matter.

不似美國，特定物履行法律並無限制。

14. The civil procedure law was enacted by the legislative branch.
    民事訴訟法由立法機關制定。

15. Taiwan does not adopt Amicus Curiae.
    無法庭之友書狀。

第三節　習題

一、選擇題（四選一）

1. Every Litigant has _____ right to appeal.
   (1) no
   (2) a
   (3) automatic
   (4) not necessarily a

2. _____ means that in order to bring a suit, the plaintiff should have a serious interest in a case, which they have sustained or are likely to sustain a direct and substantial injury from the opposing party.
   (1) Capacity
   (2) Interest at stake
   (3) Standing to sue
   (4) Interest

3. Any party can serve as a witness, if _____.
   (1) he wants
   (2) necessary
   (3) the other party requests
   (4) the judge demands

4. Attorney for both parties may raise objection on _____.

    (1) depends the situation

    (2) pretrial

    (3) during trial

    (4) during trial and even in deposition

5. Evidence should be _____, competent and material.

    (1) essential

    (2) important

    (3) relevant

    (4) to the point

6. The appellate court _____ summon new witness and admit new evident.

    (1) does not

    (2) used to

    (3) sometimes

    (4) rarely

7. The first document submitted by the plaintiff to the court is called a _____.

    (1) summon

    (2) answer

    (3) notice

    (4) complaint

8. In U.S., the legal process are basically delivered by _____.

    (1) mail

    (2) process server

    (3) party

    (4) other means

9. The judge _____ ask questions to witness.

    (1) had better not

    (2) must not

    (3) never

    (4) let the attorney

10. When the judges says "over ruled", he means that the witness _____

    __.

    (1) need not to answer

    (2) must answer

    (3) better to answer

    (4) can do either way

11. In appellate court procedure, jury are _____ used.

    (1) rarely

    (2) often

    (3) not

    (4) once in a while

12. Reverse a judgment are based on _____.

    (1) legal error

    (2) all errors

    (3) important legal error

    (4) fact not clear

13. In U.S. litigation, expert witness are _____.

    (1) chosen and paid by the party

    (2) designated by the judge

    (3) agreed by the opposing party

    (4) designated by appellate court

14. The disposition refers to testimony taken _____ from witness.

    (1) in court

    (2) outside the court

    (3) taken in emergency

    (4) through third party

15. In civil case, The American judges play a _____ role.

    (1) negative

    (2) affirmative

    (3) ordinary

    (4) special

16. In order to win a civil case the plaintiff should prove _____.

    (1) beyond a reasonable doubt

    (2) by preponderance of evidence

    (3) at the discretion of the judge

    (4) other standards

17. Interrogatories may be sent to _____.

    (1) a third party

    (2) opposing party + third party

    (3) no such thing

    (4) opposing party only

18. Injunction means a remedy to order the defendant to _____.

    (1) do an affirmative act

    (2) to refrain from doing an act

    (3) either one (1 or 2)

    (4) pay the damages

19. The effect of Appeal is generally to _____.

    (1) stop execution of the judgment

    (2) try to stop execution

    (3) stop, but up to the judge

    (4) continue to execute unless the losing party post a bond

20. Challenge prospective jurors for cause can be allowed for _____ persons.

    (1) 3

    (2) a certain number of

    (3) unlimited

    (4) as determined by the judge

21. In civil cases, the filing fee is _____.

    (1) based on the amount of subject matter

    (2) the same (uniform)

    (3) decided by the judge

    (4) decided by the parties

22. In U.S. ordinarily the trial is held _____.

    (1) many times

    (2) only once

    (3) take a long time

    (4) none

23. The aim of discovery is _____.

    (1) to assemble evidence

    (2) to find what the opposite party is doing

    (3) to intimidate the witness

    (4) to harass the opposing party

24. _____ is granted by the Supreme Court to permit the appellate party to appeal his case to that court.

    (1) Writ of execution

    (2) Writ of certiorari

    (3) Writ of mandamus

    (4) Writ of habeas corpus

25. While most civil cases are handled in state courts, federal courts handle federal question cases and _____.

    (1) domestic cases

    (2) claim cases

    (3) military cases

    (4) diversity citizenship cases

26. _____ lawsuits provide legal relief to large numbers of individuals who were wronged by a corporation and only suffered relatively small monetary losses.

    (1) Multi plaintiffs

    (2) Joint

    (3) Jointer

    (4) Class action

27. Civil contempt sanctions typically _____ when the party in contempt complies with the court order, or when the underlying case is resolved.

    (1) work

    (2) operate

    (3) start

    (4) end

▲選擇題解答

1. (4)	2. (3)	3. (1)	4. (4)	5. (3)	6. (1)	7. (4)	8. (2)	9. (1)
10. (1)	11. (3)	12. (3)	13. (1)	14. (2)	15. (1)	16. (2)	17. (4)	18. (3)
19. (4)	20. (3)	21. (2)	22. (2)	23. (1)	24. (2)	25. (4)	26. (4)	27. (4)

二、是非題

1. While federal courts handle fewer cases than most state courts, the cases heard tend to be of great importance and of great interest to the press and the public.
2. In U.S. there may be many hearings before the trial.
3. Motions are similar to our request or application.
4. The judge can always ask questions to witnesses.
5. Injunction is like our「假扣押處分」。
6. Federal court has the power to hear a civil case if the amount in controversy exceeds $75,000 and meet other requirements.

▲是非題解答
1. ○ 2. ○ 3. ✕ 4. ✕ 5. ○ 6. ○

第四節　詞彙整理

一、同義詞

govern－provide
file－submit－submit－file－present－offer
confidential－non-disclosure
privilege－power
waiver－abandonment－disclamation
cite－quote
elicit－extract
appear－attend

stay－stop
court－venue－jurisdiction
remit－remand
based on－on the ground that
maintain－argue－contend－reiterate－allegations
available－obtainable
present－demonstrate－show－introduce
grant－permit

questioning－interrogation
credit－credibility
perjury－false testimony
summation－in sum up－summary
disprove－rebuttal
to the effect－in that
bar－loss－lapse－forfeiture
defense－deny
admission－confession
process－procedure－proceeding

fair－unbiased
assert－allege－maintain－urge
confirm－certify－endorse
pending－undecided
judged－determined
proof－evidence－testimony－
　deposition
objection－protest－contest－rebut
allege－assert－claim

二、類似詞

code－statutes－law－act－
　regulation－by-laws－guidance－
　provision－decree
sue－suit－lawsuit
bring an action－institute proceeding
ligation－litigant－litigious
oppose－opponent－adversary－
　opposing party
preliminary examination－
　injunction－restraining order
amend－revise
apply－applicable
attorney－counsel－associate
clerk of the court－law clerk－
　paralegal
dismiss－drop－withdraw
reverse－reversal

claim－plead－pleading
motion－application－apply－
　request
self help－self defense－
res judicata－final－and binding
jurisdiction－power
transcript－exhibits
dismiss－defeat－reverse－remit
issues－contention－argument－
　dispute－controversy
corroborate－support－assist
judgment by default－withdraw
admit－admission－confess－
　confession
expert witness－witness
intimidate－influence
challenge－contest

remit－reverse

subpoena－summons－warrant

brief－summary

instance－level

statue of limitation－lapse

lawyer's fee－contingent fee

hearsay evidence－circumstantial
evidence

三、反義詞

bench; bar

bar; bar association; disbar

affirm; deny; reject; disprove; decline

Im rem; Im persona

plaintiff; defendant; adversary

appeal; appellant; appellee; respondent

四、詞性轉換

動詞 → 名詞

impeach → impeachment

deliver → delivery

deliberate → deliberation

| 第十章 | 刑事訴訟法 |

第一節　美國法

一、特色

1. The U.S. does not have private prosecution or civil action attached to criminal process like our law.
   公民不可追訴犯罪，美國與我國不同，並無自訴制度或附帶民事訴訟制度。

2. The U.S. adopts adversary system rather than inquisitorial system.
   美國採當事人對立主義而非糾問主義。

3. The accused may be prosecuted or punished by both federal and state courts for the same act.
   被告之同一犯罪行為可能同時受州與聯邦法律之追訴與判罪。

4. They have legal aid system and public defender system for the protection of human rights of the accused.
   有法律扶助及公設辯護制度保障被告人權。

5. Before questioning the police should inform the accused Miranda warning.
   員警盤問被告前，應告知其享有米蘭達（Miranda）等案所定之權利。

6. The accused has a lot of human right protections including no self-incrimination as well as privileges of non-disclosure of certain speeches, etc.
   被告人權保護多，包括不可命其自證其罪等，又有不透露談話之特權（包括憲法）。

7. Evidence rules are very strict. Illegally obtained evidences are not allowed.

證據法則嚴格，違法取得之證據無效。

8. In arraignment the judge may directly convict the accused and eliminate 90% cases. While this mechanism saves judicial resources but may cause human right problem.

在提審程序＊，法官可因被告答稱有罪逕行判刑，解決了90%的案件，固然可大省司法資源，但人權維護方面則不無問題。

＊在法院提審，被告可答覆有罪或無罪。

9. Before verdict the parties may enter into plea bargaining (may involve human right problem) so that only about 10% cases are finally tried by the court.

在下裁決前，當事人可締結認罪協商（也有人權問題），致法官真正審理案件數量僅占10%左右。

10. The accused may request the court to conduct jury trial.

被告可要求法官舉行陪審審理。

11. Before trial the defense, prosecutor and the judge should hold pretrial conference. The defense may request the prosecutor discovery of evidence.

在審理前，辯護律師、檢察官與法官要舉行預審會議，辯方可要求檢方證據開示。

12. In trial both parties may use cross examination to question the opposed party's witness and try to rule out false testimony.

審理時，檢辯雙方可透過交互詰問對方所提證人，以發現不實證言。

13. Unlike our system, experts are called expert witnesses who are offered and played by each party.

鑑定人稱為專家證人，由被告自行物色負擔，與我國不同。

14. In recent years in order to decrease the diversity of sentencing, the U.S. government has promulgated sentence guidelines, thus inevitably restricting judges' discretion.

近年來政府爲法官科刑定有量刑基準，減少判決歧異，當然也限制了法官的量刑權。

15. The time of sentencing may be announced later.

宣布刑罰之時間可能另定，不似我國刑罰與判決同時宣布。

16. If found guilty the accused may make appeal while the prosecutor cannot appeal if found not guilty.

如認定有罪，被告可上訴。但檢方不可對無罪上訴（一事不再理），與我國不同。

17. In recent years the judgment may order the accused to pay the victim damages or render social service or order him to receive medical treatment.

近年來判決可命被告支付賠償金（致民刑分立界限模糊）、執行社區服務及因心理健康問題接受治療。

二、內容

1. A defendant can be charged and convicted under both federal and state systems. The elements and penalty vary from one state to another.

美國爲聯邦國家，被告之同一犯罪可能同時受州與聯邦法律之追訴與判罪，而各州之犯罪構成要件與刑罰亦不相同。

2. The federal rules for criminal trials can be found in the Federal Rules of Criminal Procedure and each state has its own similar rules. The criminal justice system in the U.S. utilizes two types of juries-trial juries and grand juries.

聯邦刑事審理之規則定在聯邦刑事訴訟規則內，各州亦有自己類似的規則。*美國有大陪審與小陪審。

* 不似我國刑訴法係由立法機關制定。美國聯邦刑事訴訟規則係由聯邦最高法院受國會之授權所制定。

3. The constitution contains many provisions concerning criminal procedure, including due process of laws, equal protection, right to counselor, confront with witness, jury trial, no self-incrimination. These provisions are also applicable to all states except grand jury.
美國憲法有許多有關刑事訴訟之規定，包含保障正當法律程序、平等保護、由律師辯護、與證人對質、陪審審判及不自證犯罪等。這些規定，除大陪審外，也適用於各州。

4. The government monopolizes the prosecution of crimes. No citizen can prosecute crimes. They adopts adversary system rather than inquisitorial system.
美國由政府獨占犯罪之追訴，公民不可追訴犯罪*。美國採當事人對立主義而非糾問主義。

* 美國與我國不同，並無自訴制度或附帶民事訴訟制度。

（一）The Steps of Criminal Proceedings 刑事訴訟之步驟

1. A criminal investigation is initiated by law enforcement.
由執法機構發動刑事調查。

2. The defendant may be arrested or summoned into court and charged with a crime or crimes.
被告可能被控罪名*、被逮捕，或傳喚出庭。

* 案情嚴重者，扣留等待提審。案件輕微者，警方將其釋放，發出庭傳票，告知在指定日期出庭。

3. At an initial court hearing (arraignment) the defendant may enter a plea of guilty or not guilty or may ask for a continuance.
在法院提審，被告可答覆有罪或無罪，或請求繼續辦理。

4. The prosecution provides discovery.
檢方提供證據（開示資料）予辯方。

5. File motions prior to trial and hold pretrial conference.
在審理前提出聲請，召開預審會議。

6. A jury is selected.
選出陪審團。

7. The trial takes place.
舉行審理。

8. Any time before the verdict is delivered, the parties may enter into a plea agreement.
在下裁決前，當事人可締結認罪協商。

9. A verdict is delivered by a judge or jury.
法官或陪審團下裁決。

10. If the defendant is found guilty, then sentencing will take place.
如被告被判有罪，則進行處刑。

11. If found guilty, the defendant may appeal.
如被判罪，被告可上訴。

（二）**Rights of the Accused 被告之權利**

A criminal investigation is initiated by law enforcement. They may execute search warrants. If the accused is questioned by police, he should be advised of his constitutional right:

刑事偵查由執法機關發動。他們可發搜索票。員警盤問被告前，應告知其享有下列憲法上權利：

1. You have the right to remain silent.
你有權保持沉默。

2. Anything you say can and will be used against you in a court of law.
任何你所說的將在法庭針對你。

3. You have the right to an attorney.
你有權請律師。

4. If you cannot afford an attorney, one will be appointed for you.

Violation can lead to the exclusion of evidence from a criminal trial, possibly extinguish or weaken the case against the defendant.

如你無力請律師，可指派一人給你*。如有違反，可能導致證據在刑事法庭被排除、打消或削弱檢方控被告之案件。

　* 來自米蘭達一案判決。

（三）Arrest & Custody 逮捕與羈押

If probable cause has been established that a crime has been committed, the accused* may be arrested or summoned into court. If he is arrested, he will be taken into custody and transported to a jail. He must be transmit to court within a time limit for arraignment.

　如證明被告有相當原因犯罪，可予以逮捕，或傳喚到庭。如被逮捕，則予以羈押送入監牢，但須於期限內將被告送法院提審。

*被告之英文詞彙在民事訴訟只用 defendant，在刑訴法，除常用 accused 外，亦有用 defendant 者，二者似被混用，不加區別。

（四）Arraignment 提審

1. In a courtroom, the accused is informed the charges at this first court appearance, known as arraignment and receive a copy of the charging document. The accused then enters a plea of guilty or not guilty or may ask for a continuance. He has a right to have an attorney present. If he cannot afford an attorney, the court may appoint one at no cost.

第一次出庭，稱爲提審*，由基層法官告知被告罪名並給他一份控訴書**。然後問被告是否認罪。被告可答稱認罪或不認罪，或請求繼續進行。他有權由律師在場，如無力請律師，法院會指定免費律師。

　* 提審爲美國一種特殊制度。

**被告會收到告訴狀（information）或大陪審團之起訴書（indictment）。美國有定罪陪審（小陪審）與起訴陪審（大陪審）之分：大陪審團係由23個公民組成，進行祕密訊問。而起訴則尚有大陪審與檢察官△二元制度併用（美國檢察官對犯罪追訴有重大控制權）。

△聯邦檢察官隸屬司法部，部長（檢察總長）由總統任命參議院通過。聯邦地方法院檢察長稱為 U.S. attorneys，亦由總統任命參議院通過。

2. At the time of the arraignment, the courts will also set the amount of bail, refuse bail to the defendant, or release an individual on their own recognizance. This process can eliminate 90% cases as result of guilty pleas. Once a plea of not guilty is entered, a trial date will be set.

提審時法官也決定保釋金數額，或不准交保，或於被告承諾自行到庭後釋放。此程序可因被告答稱有罪*而排除90%的案件。一旦被告答稱不認罪，法官會定下審理日。

* 此時法官可據以逕行判刑。此種措施固然節省不少司法資源，但自人權維護言，則不無問題，因答稱有罪，實際不必然成立犯罪。

（五）Pre-trial Proceedings 審理前程序

Pre-trial proceedings allow the accused to request suppression of evidence under the exclusionary rule and resolve other matters. The defense can persuade a prosecutor to dismiss or drop charges for weak evidence, illegally obtained evidence, procedural and administrative errors.

在審理前程序，被告可依排除證據原則，請求排除證據及解決其他問題。辯護律師可以證據不足、不法取得證據及程序與行政失誤，說服檢察官撤回追訴。

（六）Discovery 證據開示

The accused is entitled to receive copies of all police reports, victim, the accused and witness statements etc. The defense may examine evidence that the government plans to introduce at trial. This must be accomplished prior to trial. Generally, the prosecution is not entitled to discovery from the defense.

被告有權收到所有警方報告影本、被害人、被告與證人之筆錄等。辯方可檢查檢方計畫在審理庭提出之證據*（須在審理前完成）。通常檢方不可要求辯方開示證據。

＊此數點為我刑訴法所無。

（七）Pretrial Motions 審理前聲請

Pretrial motions may be filed by either the defense or the prosecution, involving the introduction of evidence to be resolved prior to trial including: motions to suppress or exclude certain evidence (including physical evidence and confessions); motions to determine whether an expert is qualified to testify; motions to dismiss the case.

辯方或檢方可就審理前須解決之證據，提出審理前聲請。包括排除一些證據（包括物證與自認）、聲請決定某專家是否有資格作證，或聲請駁回該案。

（八）Pretrial Conference 預審會議

Before a trial commences, there will be a meeting of the defense, the prosecution, and the judge (pretrial hearing, sometimes called a pretrial conference). The judge can punish any party who does not appear. At the conference, the judge and the lawyers can review the evidence and clarify the issues in dispute. Judges also use pre-trial conferences to encourage settling cases.

在審理前，辯護律師、檢察官與法官要舉行會議（預審庭訊，有時稱爲預審會議）。法官可處罰不出席之一方。在會議中法官與律師可檢討證據、澄清爭點。法官亦可用預審會議鼓勵雙方將案件解決*。

*被告也須出席，檢辯雙方討論是否可免開審理而解決案件。由於可能成立認罪協商，致在審理前又有不少案件被檢察官撤回。

（九）Dismiss the Case 駁回起訴

Hearings on pretrial motions take place prior to trial. If a motion to dismiss the case is granted by the judge, the trial will not take place.

在審理前對所提聲請舉行庭訊，如法官准許駁回案件之聲請，則不舉行審理。

（十）Jury Trial 陪審審判

Defendants have a constitutional right to a jury trial. If he elects a jury trial, a jury for a felony consist of 12 members. Attorneys for both sides have "voir dire", asking a juror questions to determine if he will be impartial. Jurors can be challenged "for cause"－a legally recognized reason; or, each side can exercise a limited number of "peremptory challenges" not have to state a reason.

被告依憲法有受陪審審判之權*。如他選擇陪審審判，重罪由12人組成陪審團。雙方之律師可向候選陪審員發問，以確定他是否公正。候選陪審員可被附理由拒卻，每造亦可實施有限量之不附理由拒卻。

*刑事訴訟相關人之特權與民事訴訟相同。

（十一）Trial 審理

At the trial the prosecutor and the defense attorney deliver an opening statement to the jury (a preview of the case). The prosecution which has the burden of proving guilt (proving the case beyond a reasonable doubt) presents its evidence and witnesses first. His witnesses are subject to cross-examination by defense. Then the defense call witnesses and introduce evidence to rebut the state's claims. All defense witnesses (including the defendant if he testifies) will be subject to cross-examination by the prosecution.

在審理時，檢察官與辯方律師對陪審團發表開場說明。檢方有舉證責任（證明犯罪超過合理懷疑），首先提出證據與證人。他的證人由辯方交互詰問。然後辯方傳證人，提出證據，駁斥檢方主張。所有辯方證人由檢方交互詰問。

（十二）Privilege 特權

The Fifth Amendment of the Constitution establishes the privilege against self-crimination in order to prevent the government from forcing a person to testify against himself so that the state must prove its case without the help of the accused. During the trial, the judge maintains order and makes rulings on a variety of issues (whether evidence is admissible; or whether a question being asked of a witness is proper).

被告依憲法第五修正條文有不能自證其罪（self-incrimination）之保障＊，以防止政府迫人自證其罪，使國家不靠被告協助而須證明該案成立犯罪。法官在審理時維持秩序、對許多爭議下裁示（如證據是否可採、問證人之問題是否適當）。
＊上述保障及被告可自願作證，此二點亦與我國法不同。

（十三）Verdict 裁決

Any time before the verdict is delivered, the defendant and the prosecutor, may enter into a plea agreement—agrees to plead guilty to a charge (carry a lighter sentence than the original charge). The judge or jury determines a verdict. If the jury cannot reach a unanimous verdict, the court may declare a mistrial. If the defendant is found guilty, the court determines a sentence separately. Potential sentences may include probation, prison/jail time, and fines. If found guilty, the defendant may appeal. "Double jeopardy" (being tried twice for the same crime) prevents the prosecution from appealing an acquittal.

在下裁決前，被告可與檢方訂立認罪協商，同意對被控罪名較輕之罪認罪。法官或陪審團決定裁決。如陪審團不能達成一致裁決時，法院可宣佈判決無效。如被告被認定有罪，則由法院另定刑罰[*]。刑罰可包括緩刑、徒刑期間及罰金。如認定有罪，被告可上訴。但檢方不可對無罪上訴（一事不再理）。

[*]宣布刑罰之時間另定，不似我國與判決同時宣布。

（十四）Penalty 判刑

Certain state courts set the penalty by consulting probationer's report. Certain states adopt indeterminate imprisonment. Recently federal government and many states have promulgated sentencing guidelines for their judges in imposing penalty. The accused may be ordered to pay restitution, perform community service and receive treatment for mental health issues.

有些州法院參酌觀護人之報告[*]決定刑罰。有些州採不定期徒刑。近年來聯邦政府與許多州為法官科刑定有量刑基準。且被告可能被命支付賠償金[**]、執行社區服務及因心理健康問題接受治療。

[*]此種報告又稱為判刑前報告（pre-sentence report）。

[**]按美國近年來異於傳統之刑事處置漸多。刑事判決命被告支付償金一點，尤其與我國制度不同。

（注）本文參考

1. The Legal Process In The United States: A Criminal Case
   https://aldf.org/article/the-legal-process-in-the-united-states-a-criminal-case/
2. Criminal Procedure
   https://www.law.cornell.edu/wex/criminal_procedure
3. Criminal Defense Process: Part Two
   https://www.lawfirms.com/resources/criminal-defense/criminal-defense-case/criminal-process-two.htm
4. Criminal Arraignment: What to Expect
   By Lauren Baldwin, https://www.criminaldefenselawyer.com/resources/criminal-defense/criminal-defense-case/criminal-arraignment-what-expect

二、詞彙

summoned：傳喚

arraignment hearing：答覆認罪與否之庭訊

questioning and interrogation：盤問或與詰問

remain silent：保持緘默

exclusion of evidence：排除證據

probable cause：相當理由

questioning and interrogation：盤問與詰問

bail：保釋金

search warrant：搜索票

prosecutor：檢察官

confront witness：與證人對質

speedy trial：速審

double jeopardy：一事不再理

rebut or contradict：反駁

take the ... witness stand：作證

rebuttal evidence：反駁證據

criminal proceeding：刑事訴訟

bill of information：起訴書

proceed：進行

indicted：被起訴

indictment：起訴

plea bargain：認罪協商

charge：罪名

confession：自認

circumstantial evidence：情況證據

hearsay：傳聞證據

closing arguments：終結辯論

verdict of guilty：有罪裁決

unanimously：一致

prosecution：檢方

grand jury：大陪審團

preliminary hearing：初審、預審

plead：答覆

magistrate：治安法官

Miranda Warning：米蘭達警告

illegal search and seizure：違法搜索與扣押

victim：被害人

opening statement：開場陳述

expert testimony：專家證言

physical evidence：物證

dismiss：駁回

proceeds：進而

cross-examined：被交互詰問

opposing side：對我方

while testifying：在作證時

peremptory challenge：不附理由之淘汰（陪審員）

prison term：在監獄行刑期間

impeach the credibility of the witness：挑戰證人之信憑力

required to：需要⋯⋯

self-incriminate：使自己陷於刑責

summarizing：綜合

guilt or innocence：有罪或無辜

deliberation：評議

burden of proof：舉證責任

beyond a reasonable doubt：超越合理懷疑

commit：犯了

deadlocked：僵局

hung jury：棄置陪審團

verdict：裁決

overrule：推翻

sentencing：處刑

The United States Sentencing Commission：聯邦處刑委員會

promulgated guidance：制定的指南

assessed：評估

penalty phase：刑罰部分

imposed：科處

take the stand：作證

outcome of his trial：審理結果

appellate courts：上訴法院

retry：重審

dismissal：駁回

charge：指控

acquittal：無罪

appeal：上訴

collateral consequences of criminal charges：刑事罪名之附隨結果

parole：假釋

probation：緩刑

indeterminate imprisonment：不定期刑

community service：社區服務

rehabilitation：更生

state penitentiary：州感化院

the accused：被告

arrest：逮捕

a pool：人力庫

irrelevant, immaterial and incompetent：無關、不重要與不適格

presumption of innocence：推定無辜

adjourns：延期

deliberate in private：私下評議

craft a sentence：定刑

rehabilitation：更生

state penitentiary：州感化院

第二節　我國法

一、特色

1. Judges and prosecutors are all government appointed.
   我國法官與檢察官均由官派，不似美國刑事司法權責分散，執法機關之重要角色（許多州的法官與檢察長）由民選產生。

2. The responsibility of judges in the three levels of courts is overly heavy.
   美國刑事審判基本由一審負責，而我國三審負擔都沉重。

3. No Miranda warning is available.

我國法不採米蘭達（Miranda）警告。

4. We adopt free evaluation of evidence principle.

證據採自由心證主義，不似美國採法定證據主義。

5. The accused cannot serve as witness.

被告不能作證人。

6. Not many constitutional right for the accused compares to that of the U.S.

被告不似美國享有那麼多憲法上保障，包括免提證言（含免於自證其罪）之保障。

7. No arraignment system like that of U.S. There are too many judges especially in the Supreme Court.

沒有美國之提審制度（arraignment），不能淘汰許多案件，致案件負荷沉重。最高法院法官人數眾多。

8. No sentencing guidelines.

不似美國有量刑基準。

9. Legal aid are still in the process of to be fully developed.

近年已擴大平民法律扶助制度。

10. Recently we have adopted plea bargaining and community service system.

已採類似美國認罪協商及社區服務制度。

11. Recently we just began to let crime victim involved in criminal procedure.

最近又擴大犯罪被害人參與及知之權利。

12. No jury system. But the government has just begun to adopt so-called citizen judge system.

無陪審制，改採國民參審制度。

13. Recently we modified criminal procedure code by increasing degree of adversary system.

晚近修改刑訴法增加當事人進行色彩。

14. No concentrated trial.

不採集中審理主義。

15. Sentencing is announced with the judgment.

刑罰與判決一起宣布。

16. Judgment of court of first trial is subject to appeal or retrial perhaps many times, sometimes by prosecutor.

不似美國原則上第一審完畢即定讞，會一再上訴甚至再審，檢方對判決不滿亦可上訴。

二、詞彙

public defenders：公設辯護人

initiate public prosecutions on behalf of the state：代國家提起公訴

file private prosecutions：提起自訴

summons：傳票

domicile or residence of the accused：被告之住所或居所

appearance：出庭

warrant of arrest：拘票

commissioned judge：受命法官

stage of investigation：偵查階段

presumed to be innocent：推定無辜

final conviction：最後定讞

bear the burden of proof：負舉證責任

guilty：有罪

dismiss：駁回

Judgment of "Case Not Established"：不受理之判決

pronounced：宣示

expert witness：鑑定人

subpoenaed：傳喚

defense attorney：辯護律師

question：詢問

opposing party：對造

cross examination：交互詰問

the presiding judge：審判長

torture：刑求

allegations of police brutality：聲稱警察刑求

confessions：自白

capital punishment：死刑

dropped significantly：大爲減少

executions：執行

第三節　習題

選擇題（四選一）

1. Any time _____ the accused and the prosecutor may enter into a plea agreement.

   (1) before the sentence is delivered

   (2) before the verdict is delivered

   (3) before indictment

   (4) before judgment is rendered

2. Miranda warning should be given before _____.

   (1) before arrest

   (2) before indictment

   (3) before police interrogation

   (4) before search

3. _____ is often inadmissible at trial. The reason is simple: one cannot cross examine the person who is making the statement since that person is not in court. The person in court is simply repeating what someone else said.

(1) Irrelevant evidence

(2) Hearsay evidence

(3) Immaterial evidence

(4) Confession

4. An accused may only seek _____ obtained in violation of the accused's own rights. Evidence against the accused obtained in a warrantless search of someone else's home may not be subject to suppression by the defendant.

(1) suppression of evidence

(2) confession

(3) admission

(4) "Fruit of the poisonous tree"

5. If _____ has been established that a crime has been committed, the defendant may be arrested or summoned into court.

(1) probable cause（相當原因）

(2) no cause

(3) certain cause

(4) definite cause

6. At these hearings, the defense may request that the accused be granted _____ or that the court reduce the amount of bond.

(1) a personal recognizance bond

(2) guaranty

(3) surety

(4) security

7. Once _____, a trial date will be set.

   (1) a plea of not guilty is enter

   (2) defendant appears before the court

   (3) arraignment is complete

   (4) the prosecutor decides

8. The accused is entitled to receive _____ from the prosecution.

   (1) copies of all police reports

   (2) no such copies

   (3) certain reports

   (4) his oral report only

9. The prosecution has the burden of proving guilt _____.

   (1) beyond a reasonable doubt

   (2) clear & convincing evidence

   (3) preponderance of evidence

   (4) by free assessment of evidence

10. All witnesses are subject to _____ by the other party.

   (1) cross-examination

   (2) direct examination

   (3) redirect examination

   (4) examination

11. If the jury cannot reach a unanimous verdict, the court may declare

   _____.

   (1) retrial

   (2) a mistrial

   (3) new trial

   (4) reopen

12. If the accused elects a jury trial, attorneys for both sides can ask a juror questions to determine if he will be impartial. This is called _____.

    (1) selection

    (2) voir dire

    (3) examination

    (4) test

13. If the accused is found not guilty, _____ prevents the prosecution from appealing.

    (1) evidence

    (2) "Double jeopardy" (being tried twice for the same crime)

    (3) verdict

    (4) judgment

14. In some courts, the accused may be ordered by the judge to pay _____ to the victim.

    (1) fine

    (2) restitution

    (3) destitution

    (4) bribe

15. _____ is an illegal measure to collect evidence.

    (1) Confession

    (2) Wiretapping

    (3) Finger print

    (4) Booking

16. Generally, _____ questioning is not allowed during the trial.

    (1) cross

    (2) indirect

    (3) redirect

    (4) leading

17. The defense may try to abate the value of an expert witness by __
    ____.
    (1) objection
    (2) impeaching his credibility
    (3) denying
    (4) more questioning

18. A government can reciprocally request foreign government to hand
    over a criminal called _____.
    (1) transfer
    (2) distortion
    (3) extradition
    (4) exchange

19. The Fifth Amendment of the U.S. Constitution grants the privilege
    _____ in order to prevent the government from forcing a person
    to testify against himself. Consequently the state must prove its
    case without the help of the accused.
    (1) of keeping silence
    (2) against self-incrimination
    (3) against incrimination
    (4) of freedom

▲選擇題解答

1. (2)	2. (3)	3. (2)	4. (1)	5. (1)	6. (1)	7. (1)	8. (1)	9. (1)
10. (1)	11. (2)	12. (2)	13. (2)	14. (2)	15. (2)	16. (4)	17. (2)	18. (3)
19. (2)								

第四節　詞彙整理

一、類似詞

catastrophe－famine－war－act of god－force majure

primarily－generally－as a rule－regularly

fact－truth

mitigate－exonerate

reveal－discover

kill－murder－manslaughter－massacre－genocide－homicide

set aside－dismiss

kidnapping－false imprisonment

steal－robbery－larceny－burglary

indictment－information

intent－intention－intended

negligent－gross negligent－willful－reckless－malicious－extreme－extraordinary

harm－injury－loss－hurt

obstruction－impede－hinder

arson－vandalism－destruction

nuisance－disturbance－intrusion－trespass

coercion－duress

provocation－cause

unreasonable－unfair

discretion－power－sovereignty

construct－interpret－construe

forgery－counterfeiting

spiritual－mental－mentality

drug－narcotics

abet－teach－instruct－encourage

forgive－forego－condone

accuser－prosecutor

defender－public defender－pro bono

accuse－complain

excuse－justification

judgment－order－ruling－verdict－award－sentence－conviction

enter－deliver－found

impose－charge

parole－probation－release－suspend execution－indeterminate sentence

restraining order－injunction

custody－arrest－detain－detention

review－appeal

guideline－rule

questioning－interrogation

force－strength

二、反義詞

affirmative; negative   exonerate; aggravate

true; false

三、詞性轉換

動詞 → 名詞

foresee → foreseeability   forfeit → forfeiture

第十一章　　法律倫理

第一節　美國法

一、介紹

The American Bar Association has promulgated the Model Rules of Professional Conduct which have been influential in many jurisdictions. The Model Rules address many topics which are adopted in many state ethics rules. Failure to obey these rules may subject a lawyer to sanction.

在美國大學法學院近年須開職業責任課程，包含法律倫理及一般專業事務。律師考試亦在考試之列。律師被認爲在野法曹，法曹協會自夙勢力強大。各州法曹協會常諮詢法院後定下一套倫理義務。美國法曹協會訂有模範職業行爲規則。雖然美國法曹協會是民間機構，欠缺對任何人課規則之權力，但該模範規則已由許多州定爲法律。不遵守當地倫理規則之律師可能受到懲戒。

（一）Model Rules of Professional Conduct 律師之職業行爲規則

Pursuant to the Model Rules, a lawyer has the following duties:
依該模範規則律師主要有下列義務：

1. Duty of Competent Representation 勝任代理之義務

An attorney must refrain from representing clients or associate with a knowledgeable one or adequately prepare, if he does not have enough knowledge or experience.

若無充分知識或經驗處理事務，則不接受代理，或與對代理主題有研究之律師合作，或作充分之準備。

2. Duty to Consult 諮詢之義務

An attorney must make unilateral decision without obtaining consent from his clients.

就進行方法諮詢當事人，如和解。刑事方面，當事人是否作證，答覆有罪或放棄陪審等，非經當事人同意，不可片面決定影響當事人之實體權利。

3. Duty of Diligence 勤勉之義務

An attorney must take action to purse matters without delay on behalf of his clients regardless difficulties.

不管大眾反對或個人不便，應認真與快速代理當事人，避免遲誤。

4. Duty to Charge Reasonable Fees 收取合理費用

An attorney must charge reasonable fees and communicate with his clients in due time. Contingent fee are not allowed in domestic matters or criminal cases.

費用應於開始代理後之合理時間，以書面通知當事人。禁止在家事案件與刑事案件，收取成功報酬。

5. Duty of Loyalty and Conflicts of Interest 忠實之義務

An attorney must not represent clients when there is a conflict of interest between him and the client. If he has a client whose interests are adverse to those of a potential client, decline the second representation.

當律師個人利益與當事人利益衝突時，不可代理。又如已有一當事人其利益反於一個潛在當事人時，須拒絕第二個代理。

6. Duty of Confidentiality 保密之義務

An attorney must not disclose information relating to client matters unless having client's consent.

除非諮詢當事人或有默示授權，不可透露有關代理當事人之資訊。

7. Duty of Candor to the Court 對法院正直之義務

As officer of the court, the duty to the court and general public takes priority over the duty to his client.

對公眾與法院之義務優先於其對當事人之義務。

8. Duties to the Profession and Others 對職業與公眾之義務

An attorney must do pro bono service at least 50 hours per year and refrain from solicitation. His advertisement should be truthful.

每年宜撥50小時以上為平民服務（pro bono service），且禁止招攬業務，廣告內容要實在。

9. Duty to Refrain from Asserting Frivolous Claims 不應提微不足道之訴訟*

An attorney must not bring frivolous claims unless they are based on good faith.

除基於善意外，不應提出微不足道之訴訟。

*參照 Burnham, Introduction to the law and legal System of the United States (Thomson/West, 2006) p.159 et seq.

（二）Code of Conduct for United States Judges 美國法官行為守則

Canon 1: A judge shall uphold and promote the integrity and independence of the judiciary.

1.法官應維護並促進司法界之正直與獨立。

Canon 2: A judge should avoid impropriety and the appearance of impropriety in all activities.

2. 法官在所有活動應避免不當與不當之外觀。

Canon 3: A judge should perform the duties of the office fairly, impartially and diligently.

3. 法官應公開公正勤勉履行職務。

Canon 4: A judge may engage in extrajudicial activities that are consistent with the obligations of judicial office.

4. 法官得從事與司法職務符合之司法外活動。

Canon 5: A judge should refrain from political activity.

5. 法官應避免政治活動。

二、詞彙

pro bono service：公益服務

malpractice：業務過失

conflicts of interest：利益衝突

duty of candor：忠誠之義務

duty of confidentiality：保密之義務

client solicitation：招徠當事人

duty of loyalty：忠實之義務

duty of diligence：勤勉之義務

duty to consult：諮詢之義務

duty of competent representation：勝任代理之義務

duty to charge reasonable fees：收取合理費用義務

self-regulation：自律

officers of the court：法院之官員

undivided loyalty：忠貞不二

contingent fee：成功報酬

American Bar Association：美國法曹協會（或譯美國律師公會）

impropriety：不當情事

appearance：外觀

impartially：公正

uphold：維護

integrity：正直

extrajudicial Activities：司法以外活動

consistent with：符合

refrain from：避免

disciplinary procedeeing：懲戒程序

law firm：聯合律師事務所

law school：法律學院

courts of limited jurisdiction：有限管轄權之法院

presided over：主持

general jurisdiction trial courts：有一般管轄權之審判法院

traffic or family law cases：交通或家事法案件

intermediate appellate court：中間上訴法院

Chief Justice：院長

the day-to-day operations：日常運作

payroll, equipment and supplies：薪俸、設備及供應

court personnel：法院人員

The U.S. Sentencing Commission：聯邦處刑委員會

licensed：發執照

practice law：執行律務

Juris Doctor：美國法律學院第一個學位（若譯法律博士則欠當）

post-graduate degree：大學後學位

bar examination：律師考試

specialization：專門

第二節　我國法

一、律師

Lawyers should not have improper social contact with judicial personnel. They should refrain from bringing frivolous lawsuits. They should refrain from putting improper solicitation or intimidating notice. Heavy violation may constitute grounds for disciplinary actions. Lawyer Ethical Rules also stipulate that their duties towards judicial authority, clients and other lawyers such as keeping secrets, refraining from taking cases of conflict interests, almost similar to American counterparts.

律師法原有律師權利義務之規定，包含司法人員離職之日起三年內不得在原法院執行律師職務。律師不得與司法人員有不正酬應，為顯無理由之起訴上訴，不正當招攬訴訟，刊登招搖或恐嚇啟事。重大違反可能構成懲戒（含警告、申誡、停止職務及除名）之事由。律師倫理規範復規定各種義務，包含紀律，律師與司法機關，與委任人，律師相互間之各種義務，諸如嚴守秘密，不得受任與當事人利害衝突案件，大體與上述美國規範相類似。

二、法官與檢察官

Judges and prosecutors: Judges Act provides that, judges should obey judges' ethical rules as provided in the said Act. These contents are more comprehensive than the American counterpart. If violated, they may be subjected to various disciplinary actions. This Act applies mutatis mutandis to prosecutors.

法官法規定法官應遵守該法所定之法官倫理規範，內容遠較上述美國法官詳盡。如有違反，依情節可能受各種輕重懲戒處分。該法準用於檢察官。

第三節　習題

選擇題（四選一）

1. A, an attorney, sold his house to his client B. A's action could violate duty of _____.

   (1) separation of property

   (2) faithfulness

   (3) avoiding conflict interest

   (4) honesty

2. A never took a course in securities law. He boasts that he is an expert of securities law and received a case. He violates _____.

   (1) duty of disclosing

   (2) duty of competent representation

   (3) duty of preparation

   (4) duty of reporting

3. A entered into an arbitration contract on his client's behalf, with the opposing party, without getting approval from his client, he may violate _____.

   (1) duty of being modest

   (2) duty to consult

   (3) duty of reporting

   (4) duty of loyalty

4. A, an attorney, fail to submit appeal for his client in time. He is in violation of _____.

   (1) duty of representation

   (2) duty of diligence

   (3) duty of loyalty

   (4) duty of working

5. A, an attorney, brought for his client, a frivolous case against C. A may violate duty to _____.

(1) refrain from asserting frivolous claim

(2) consult

(3) work hard

(4) judicial administration

6. A, an attorney, advertised in the newspaper citing he win a case for his client B. A may violate _____.

(1) duty not to advertise

(2) duty to be modest

(3) duty to restrain

(4) duty of confidentiality

7. A, in calculating his hourly charge to his client, charge too much. He may violate _____.

(1) duty not to cheat

(2) duty to be honest

(3) duty to charge reasonable fees

(4) duty to be loyal

▲選擇題解答

1. (3)　2. (2)　3. (2)　4. (2)　5. (1)　6. (4)　7. (3)

第四節　詞彙整理

詞性轉換

（一）動詞 → 名詞

solicit → solicitation

maintain → maintenance

comply → compliance

oblige → obligation

perform → performance

（二）形容詞 → 名詞

legal → legality

ethical → ethics

candid → candor

consistent → consistence

impartial → impartiality

confidential → confidentiality

frivolous → frivolousness

loyal → loyalty

diligent → diligence

國家圖書館出版品預行編目資料

進階法學英文：從比較台美法律講起／楊
　崇森著. -- 初版. -- 臺北市：五南圖
　書出版股份有限公司, 2023.06
　面；　公分
　ISBN 978-626-366-118-9（平裝）

1.CST: 法學英語　2.CST: 讀本

805.18　　　　　　　　　112007699

1QJB

進階法學英文：
從比較台美法律講起

作　　者 ― 楊崇森（311.7）

發 行 人 ― 楊榮川

總 經 理 ― 楊士清

總 編 輯 ― 楊秀麗

副總編輯 ― 劉靜芬

責任編輯 ― 林佳瑩

封面設計 ― 陳亭瑋

出 版 者 ― 五南圖書出版股份有限公司

地　　址：106台北市大安區和平東路二段339號4樓

電　　話：(02)2705-5066　　傳　　真：(02)2706-6100

網　　址：https://www.wunan.com.tw

電子郵件：wunan@wunan.com.tw

劃撥帳號：01068953

戶　　名：五南圖書出版股份有限公司

法律顧問　林勝安律師

出版日期　2023年6月初版一刷

定　　價　新臺幣420元

經典永恆·名著常在

五十週年的獻禮 —— 經典名著文庫

五南，五十年了，半個世紀，人生旅程的一大半，走過來了。

思索著，邁向百年的未來歷程，能為知識界、文化學術界作些什麼？

在速食文化的生態下，有什麼值得讓人雋永品味的？

歷代經典·當今名著，經過時間的洗禮，千錘百鍊，流傳至今，光芒耀人；

不僅使我們能領悟前人的智慧，同時也增深加廣我們思考的深度與視野。

我們決心投入巨資，有計畫的系統梳選，成立「經典名著文庫」，

希望收入古今中外思想性的、充滿睿智與獨見的經典、名著。

這是一項理想性的、永續性的巨大出版工程。

不在意讀者的眾寡，只考慮它的學術價值，力求完整展現先哲思想的軌跡；

為知識界開啟一片智慧之窗，營造一座百花綻放的世界文明公園，

任君遨遊、取菁吸蜜、嘉惠學子！